The Price of Betrayal

By

Brenda Adcock

ISBN 978-1-61929-473-8

Cover Design by AcornGraphics

Editors Patty Schramm and Lynnette Beers

Publisher's Note:

Also by Brenda Adcock

Pipeline
Reiko's Garden
Redress of Grievances
The Sea Hawk
Tunnel Vision
Soiled Dove
The Other Mrs. Champion
The Chameleon
Picking Up the Pieces
The Game of Denial
In the Midnight Hour Untouchable
The Heart of the Mountain
Gift of the Redeemer Unresolved Conflicts
One Step At A Time

Chapter One

Audie Wade hadn't cruised a bar in nearly twenty-five years. Not since she was a troubled and confused eighteen-year-old kid away from home for the first time, searching for a way to come to grips with who she knew she was inside. But she wasn't really cruising this night, she told herself. She had to have a night away from home.

Watching Carlie waste away day after day was too much, and she needed to escape, if only for a few hours. She'd already been to two other bars...or was it three? She didn't remember. It didn't matter.

She rested her elbows on the bar and motioned to the woman behind it. "Double bourbon, neat," she said, dropping a twenty. She couldn't remember how many doubles she'd already consumed, but it wasn't enough to make her forget. The bartender set the glass on a napkin in front of her. Audie tossed it back before her change was counted out and set the glass down as the alcohol burned its way down her throat.

She would have to stop somewhere and grab a bite to eat before returning home. "One more," she said quietly, surveying the women sitting at the bar and in dark booths along the walls.

"Tough day?" the bartender asked with a smile as she refilled the drink.

Audie frowned grimly and sighed. "Tough year."

"Don't think I've ever seen you here before, and I'd remember a woman as tall as you, Stretch. I'm guessin' you're what, about six-feet," the bartender chatted amiably.

"Six-two," Audie answered as she sipped the fresh drink and looked around. "Slow night."

"It's a weeknight." The bartender shrugged and then drifted away to serve another thirsty customer.

Audie could feel the effects of the alcohol on her body as it succumbed to the warm glow spreading through her. She'd just needed something to take the edge off. While she watched a couple in a booth near the dance floor grope one another, she felt her stomach clench slightly. Visions of Carlie pulling her down, eager to touch her and be touched, floated across her mind's eye. God, how she missed her lover's desire, her passion.

Even after all the years they'd been together, she'd never stopped wanting Carlie. She felt like a fucking rabbit in heat every time Carlie gazed at her with that...look. A smile skimmed across her lips at the thought of Carlie drawing her closer. She hadn't known that loving someone and making love to them could cause you lose your mind until she'd met Carlie twenty years ago. The first time Audie saw Carlie, she knew the beautiful, shy young woman was meant to share her life forever.

She could feel her eyes burning and fought back the tears she knew were waiting to erupt. She shook her head in a futile attempt to clear her mind and erase the memory of all those terrible fights with her mother, a rational intellectual, but stiff-necked woman who still refused to speak to her only daughter, disgusted by how she chose to live her life. Elisha Wade was a woman who avoided making waves, and Audie had definitely made waves.

Audie noticed a woman sitting alone at the end of the bar. Now there was a possibility. She wasn't beautiful, but she was pretty enough, in an ordinary sort of way. A little more weight than Audie would have preferred, but, hell, she wasn't looking for a commitment. She needed to fuck another woman, and she hadn't ever known any that didn't have the same equipment, even if it wasn't in prime condition.

Audie pushed away from the bar, picked up the remainder of her drink, and made her way casually toward the woman, whom she could tell as she got closer was much younger than her own forty-four years. As she slid onto a stool beside her, Audie forced a smile. It had been so long since she'd attempted to pick up a woman, that she needed to think about what to do. Something simple, she thought. Simple used to work better for her than any of the inane pick-up lines she'd heard.

"Would you like a refill?" Audie asked.

The woman brushed back somewhat unruly, curly mousy

brown hair and let her eyes pass quickly over Audie. "Sure," she said and shrugged. "Thanks."

Audie signaled to the bartender and said in a low voice, "I'm Audie."

"Emily," the younger woman replied as she extended her hand. Audie couldn't help but notice the manicured nails that decorated the woman's fingers.

"Are you here alone?" Audie asked as she handed her money to the bartender for the two drinks.

"It wasn't my original plan, but yes, I guess I am…alone. Do you come here often?"

"No. Just killing time before I wander back home. Would you like to dance?"

"I'm not very good."

"Doesn't matter," Audie said with a smile she didn't quite mean. "As long as you have someone interesting in your arms."

Audie stood and held her hand out without looking at Emily, feeling the warmth as their fingers met. She led Emily to the dance floor, turned, took her into her arms, and glided slowly into the music. Emily was at least a head shorter and hadn't been lying about her dancing ability. Carlie was a graceful, accomplished dancer, almost balletic, but seductive in a way that always sneaked up on Audie when their bodies touched. Audie brought Emily's body closer, moving to brush her thigh against Emily's leg occasionally. She hated this seduction shit and hoped it wasn't going to take hours of small talk to get what she really wanted.

When the dance finally ended, Audie escorted Emily back to the bar. "Let's find a booth," Audie suggested as she took a drink of her whiskey. "Get better acquainted."

"Okay," Emily agreed shyly and picked up her drink.

Emily followed Audie toward the back of the club and into a booth. Audie slid in smoothly next to her. She was done with the pre-sex coyness. She'd had more than enough to drink, and the lack of food was making her lightheaded. She watched Emily sip her drink and brought her left arm up to rest along the top of the booth seat. Emily leaned back into the corner of the booth and took a deep breath as Audie smiled at her.

"You're very pretty," Audie lied and turned slightly to

allow her right hand to slide up Emily's thigh. She detected a small hitch in Emily's breathing but shifted her body and leaned closer, grinning when she saw Emily's eyes dart around, as if unsure what to do. Before she could give it much more thought, Audie teased her lips with a light kiss. Coolly assessing Emily's reaction, Audie ran her right hand along Emily's waist as her left found the back of Emily's neck and drew her into a deeper, probing kiss.

Audie pressed even closer, swept into a craving for more, her mouth taking Emily's aggressively as her fingers located skin and traveled to full breasts, nipples rising in anticipation. A deep groan escaped Emily's throat as Audie bit lightly at her neck and fondled her breasts. Audie was breathing heavily and was through flirting and teasing.

"Let's go somewhere more private," she whispered.

She didn't remember how they got there, but as soon as the door to the motel room closed behind them, Audie's body was humming with want, aching with need, as she began helping Emily undress between lust-filled kisses. There wasn't much to say, and Audie had no need for more small talk. Her body and her brain had only a single goal, and her hands and mouth were communicating enough.

When she pushed Emily back onto the bed and stripped her own clothes off, she noticed a tattoo encircling Emily's right bicep. "Interesting tat," she said as she joined Emily, blinking hard to clear her eyes as she lowered herself while kissing the younger woman soundly, feeling the soft body beneath her own. "Did it hurt?"

"I cried like a baby," Emily admitted as her hands ran down Audie's back.

"Don't talk," Audie said as she drew Emily up, exposing hardening nipples ripe for the taking.

"Audie…," Emily started as Audie's mouth devoured her breasts, taking a nipple between her teeth.

Within seconds, Emily's body responded to Audie's mouth sucking and pulling her breasts, teasing with the tip of her tongue.

"So…good," Emily said as she gasped, the rest of her body beginning to squirm beneath Audie's.

Audie floated her hand deftly along Emily's abdomen,

feeling the untoned muscles begin to quiver, the heels of her feet digging into the bedcovers, bringing her hips up to meet Audie's hand. Lost in what she was doing, Audie responded to every movement of Emily's body, teasing between her legs, stroking her clitoris, feeling the wetness against her hand. The smell of passionate need reached her senses, and the thought of taking the woman brought a painful knot to her own abdomen.

This wasn't Carlie. She wasn't even a good substitute, but she was willing and she was alive, and that was all that mattered. Audie pulled Emily up onto her thighs and drove her fingers into her slickness, holding her tightly.

"Oh, God!" Emily moaned, gripping Audie's shoulders as she rode the long fingers that stroked into her demandingly and relentlessly. Audie drove harder into the sweet wetness, feeling the tightness within her own body beginning to slip, but fought the feeling off. Within moments, Emily's body began to buck wildly against Audie's hand, forcing her to hold the woman closer. She wouldn't allow her to escape, so she continued to stroke boldly until Emily's body jerked into multiple waves of orgasm. Unable to control her own body any longer, Audie released Emily, pushing her down onto the bed, her fingers still stroking her slowly. She straddled Emily's thigh and whispered, "Once more, baby."

"I...I can't...I," Emily struggled. "Please...stop...I...can't."

"Yes, you can," Audie said firmly, her fingers moving into Emily's body forcefully again as she slid her own wetness along Emily's thigh. Emily's body reacted involuntarily to Audie's strokes while Audie went into her own mind, forcing herself to feel Carlie's touch again as she began to tense for the orgasm she'd suppressed for longer than she could remember.

A moment later, her body stiffened as her muscles clenched before surrendering to the hot, wet release she'd been craving.

****

Audie didn't know what time it was when her eyes flew open and she glanced around the darkened room. The woman beside her was breathing evenly, softly snoring, half covered by the cheap bargain store chenille bedspread. Red numerals blinked twelve-thirty.

Shit! How long had she been asleep? She had to get out of there and get home. *Fuck!* She swung her legs off the bed, stood, gripped the nightstand for balance, and tried to find her clothes in the darkness. She was dressed within a few minutes and stood with her hand on the doorknob to the room. She glanced at Emily sprawled on the bed and frowned. She reached into her back pocket, pulled out her wallet, and dropped a fifty on the nightstand. She should wake her and offer to take her home or back to the bar, but she didn't have time. She was ashamed and didn't want to remember her. She came, she saw, she conquered. Or maybe it should have been she saw, she conquered, and then she came.

She opened the door quietly, slipped out into the warm September night, and walked to her car. This was just a one-time thing. It would never happen again. She only needed a little relief from the despair and stress in her life. No one would ever know it happened except her and the stranger sleeping in the motel room...and Audie would never see her again.

Chapter Two

Reagan Malloy couldn't bring herself to look at the flower-covered casket that held the body of her friend. Although the weather was warm, she felt a chill run down her spine and shivered involuntarily. Tracey Chaisson wrapped her arm around Reagan's shoulders and pulled her closer. Tears trickled down Reagan's cheeks. She didn't hear anything the minister said as he eulogized the short life of Emily King, a friendly, gentle, promising young woman who never hurt anyone, leaving those who loved her too soon.

Twenty minutes later, Reagan ran a hand through her hair as she held Tracey's hand and walked toward a waiting car. Tracey slipped her shades on and looked at Reagan for a moment.

"You okay, Reagan?" she asked.

"No. Are you?" Reagan snapped.

"When was the last time you talked to her?" Tracey asked as she loosened her tie and pulled it from around her neck. "I hate these damn things. Makes me feel like I'm fuckin' strangling."

"One of the hazards of being such a serious butch, I guess." Reagan shrugged as she drew in a deep breath. She squinted up at the bright sun. "Actually, I spoke to her the day before she…died. She called, and we argued again. She was upset because I wouldn't drop everything and drive up to visit her, like I could just jump in my car and zip up to Austin every time she felt lonely or horny," she said and sniffed. "She even threatened to go out and hook up with someone else since she couldn't depend on me to rush to her side and satisfy her."

"Maybe she was just depressed. You know how she was."

"She was *always* depressed, Trace, even in high school. Between her low self-esteem and her parents' high expectations, it seemed like she spent her life fighting her weight, taking pills, or some other shit like that. She was a damn drama queen and too freakin' needy. I don't know why I even bothered going out with her."

"All she wanted was someone to love her and accept her for who she was."

"Yeah, well, you can't find a meaningful relationship by gettin' drunk and then fuckin' anyone who looks at you twice," Reagan said and frowned. "That's just plain old pathetic."

Tracey pulled off her sunglasses and glared at Reagan. "What the fuck is your problem, Reagan? Emily was your girlfriend, and now she's dead and you're bad mouthin' her!"

"She wasn't my fucking girlfriend, Tracey," Reagan snapped as she pushed her away. "Emily was a *friend*, with occasional benefits, but I'm so pissed off at her. She had so much to offer and just threw it all away. For what? To go out and pick up another total stranger who didn't give a shit about her? Just so she could get laid? I don't understand what she was thinking." Reagan sobbed the last words of her rant.

Tracey wrapped her arms around Reagan and hugged her fiercely. Reagan clung to Tracey as she thought about how she'd let Emily, her best friend since elementary school, down and forced her to turn to another woman, a stranger, for satisfaction. Now she was gone.

"Let's go somewhere and talk," Tracey said softly as she stroked Reagan's hair and kissed her gently. "Maybe have a drink or two."

"Take me back to my place so I can change first," Reagan said and wiped her eyes.

As Reagan slid into the front seat of Tracey's sedan, Tracey leaned in and said, "Maybe we can go to Big Al's for lunch. Emily liked eatin' there when she was home."

****

A little after noon, Tracey followed Reagan into Big Al's Spaghetti Factory in the warehouse district of southwest Houston. Reagan had changed into comfortable old jeans and a white scoop neck sweater, and Tracey was dressed in her usual biker jeans and Harley T-shirt over heavy, black boots. They strolled toward the back booth.

Once upon a time, Reagan, Tracey, and Emily, along with

some other girls, banded together because they were considered outside the mainstream of typical high school girls. They all dressed differently, looked outrageously Goth, and were outspoken about their disdain for following the crowd.

Out partying one night during their senior year, Reagan, a proud and adventurous young dyke, made a blatant pass at Emily which ended in intimacy, a relationship that continued off-and-on for the next several years. It never advanced to anything more serious than a pleasant diversion, except possibly in Emily's mind.

"This place brings back a lot of pretty good memories," Tracey finally said as she perused her menu.

"That was a long time ago," Reagan muttered. "We were just a bunch of dumb kids who thought we were all grown up and knew everything. But shit changes," she said and shook her head. "People change, and we never really know why."

Tracey took a deep breath. "I helped Em's folks clean out her apartment when they drove up to Austin."

"Did they tell you anything?" Reagan asked.

"Just that someone in her study group found her and called the cops. The medical examiner said it was a suicide. Pills mixed with alcohol."

I don't believe that, Reagan thought. Em was incapable of even taking a Tylenol without throwing up. Washing pills down with alcohol also seemed unlikely since the girl could nurse a single drink for hours because she wanted to stay sober so she could remember whether or not she had a good time, which she seldom did.

"There were a few bruises on her body, and they thought she'd had sex with someone, but they didn't find anything," Tracey chattered on.

"Well, there probably wouldn't have been if she was with another woman," Reagan said and snorted. "I guess she kept her threat then. Found a friendly companion to spend a night with and probably took a bath afterward."

"She called me after you two argued. She was pretty upset."

"She was always upset about something."

"Maybe your argument was the final straw."

"Are you blaming *me* for Emily's death?" Reagan snapped,

waving her hands in front of her face. "We only fucked for fun, just like we all did."

"Don't get all pissy about it, Reagan," Tracey retorted. "Maybe whoever she picked up got...carried away, and it pushed her over the edge."

"You can't be fuckin' serious!"

"All I'm sayin' is that it's possible. She told me being away from home and her friends was harder than she thought it would be. Being alone in a new town really messed with her head."

Reagan frowned and rubbed her eyes. "That it? She was the one picking up random women to fuck."

"Pretty much." Tracey nodded.

"You know how Em was. She was a pile of insecurities looking for validation, but it doesn't mean that any of the women she picked up knew she might kill herself afterward. We both know what can happen if we pick up some total stranger to get off with. It might not be the greatest experience of a lifetime, but it's usually not bad enough to cause us to want to kill ourselves afterward. You live in Austin, Trace. Did you spend much time with her?"

"I wish I had, but my job takes up most of my time, and I was usually too tired to go club-hopping with her. Now I wish I had," Tracey said. "She called the night before she killed herself, wanting me to go out with her, but I begged off."

"There probably wasn't anything any of us could have done, but she was closer to me than the rest of the group, and I'm gonna miss her like hell."

"Me, too, so let's eat at her favorite place in her memory." Tracey smiled, reaching over and squeezing Reagan's arm. "I have to get back to Austin tonight."

****

Audie gazed up at the bright blue January sky and squinted slightly behind her sunglasses. It was a cold day, but there wasn't a cloud in the sky. Carlie would have loved a day like this.

She was glad it was finally over. She'd cried so many times in the last two years and prayed for an end to Carlie's suffering. Her prayers had finally been answered; there were no more tears she could shed.

"You're free now, baby," she said softly as she gently placed a yellow rose, Carlie's favorite, on the casket and let her hand linger against the cold, smooth, walnut finish in a final caress.

A gloved hand slipped around Audie's waist. "Are you all right, Audie?" Carlie's sister asked.

Audie turned toward her and smiled slightly. "I'm fine, Lynn. We're both fine at last."

After she buttoned her calf-length black cashmere coat snugly, Audie walked toward Suzanne's car, pausing to hug and speak briefly to Carlie's parents, who had accepted her when her own parent wouldn't. Their friends gathered near the car to express their final condolences.

As Audie turned back toward the vehicle, Suzanne Travers, her friend and business partner, opened the door and hugged her briefly before she got in. It was warm inside, so Audie took a deep breath and unbuttoned her coat.

Suzanne's partner, Gianna, reached over the seat and patted Audie's knee as Suzanne shifted the vehicle into drive and slowly left the cemetery.

"I suppose you invited them all to your place," Suzanne said.

"Of course. It's mostly Carlie's family and colleagues. It's what she would have wanted." Audie frowned at the rows of headstones as they drove past them. "They all have a need to remember better times and put this behind them."

"So do you," Suzanne said as she looked at her in the rearview mirror.

"I'll be fine, Suzanne. I'm taking next week off. There are some things I need to take care of before I go back to work."

"Like what?"

"Lynn and Carlie's parents will want some of her personal belongings, and I have an appointment with a realtor to discuss putting the retreat on the coast up for sale. Shouldn't take long," Audie said, pulling off her sunglasses.

"We fly to California in two weeks. Will you be able to go?" Suzanne asked casually as she turned onto the highway.

"Audie knows what she has to do, Suzanna," Gianna said

in her distinctive Italian accent.

"I just don't want you to get bogged down with grief, Audie. Being alone can do that."

"The life I knew ended after the doctor's diagnosis, Suzanne. But don't worry. I know what my obligations are."

"I know you do, sweetie. But don't forget the most important obligation of all. The one to yourself."

Audie smiled as she looked out the side window. The warmth of the sun striking her face dredged up what seemed to be a lifetime of memories that warmed her soul. She remembered being a five-year-old riding in her father's Jeep through the New Mexico desert again, laughing as her father drove in circles churning up a red plume of dust behind them and watching it billow into the bright blue sky until it settled, leaving them covered with a fine red coating of red. She remembered fifteen years later, holding Carlie's hand, hiking in the Oklahoma hills, and basking in the sunshine of Carlie's smile when she looked at Audie, the blush of love on her face. It seemed that in a blink all those happy memories disappeared. Now all she saw were cold reminders that those warm days were gone. Would she ever find her way back into the sunshine again?

****

By the time Audie escorted the last of the well-wishers out of the home she'd shared with Carlie, she was exhausted. She would go to bed alone, sleep alone, and wake up alone. Even when Carlie was sick, Audie fell asleep holding her gently in her arms. The only difference was Carlie's scent, which changed gradually from her usual refreshing, springtime lavender to something more medicinal.

"Are you sure you don't want me to help you?" Lynn asked, snapping Audie back to the present.

Audie leaned down slightly to allow her fingertips to stroke the head of their yellow Labrador Retriever, Buck, who was pressed against her leg, providing her some degree of comfort. Carlie didn't want the dog when Audie first brought him home, but it hadn't taken him long to win her over with his soft brown eyes. In less than a month, they were buddies, and he followed Carlie everywhere, curling his body at her feet while she worked. Audie was certain Buck was grieving in his own way. "I lived with your sister for twenty-four years, Lynn. I know what she wanted done with her belongings, and honoring her final wishes is the last thing I can do for her," Audie said and sighed.

"Well, if there's anything you need me to do, please call."

"I will, Lynn. I know there are some things that Carlie wanted you to have."

"No hurry, Audie."

"I'm driving down to the coast the day after tomorrow. I'll come by when I get back."

"Taking some time off?" Lynn asked.

"I'm thinking about selling our retreat. I haven't been there in over two years. It'll probably need some work done, and I know we left personal things there that I need to bring home."

"Carlie loved it there." Lynn sighed.

"We both did." Audie smiled faintly.

"I could go if you think you'll need help," Lynn offered.

"I'm not trying to be rude, Lynn. You and Jerry and your folks have been wonderful, but I just need a little time alone." Carlie's family accepted and loved Audie as another daughter, unlike her own. She had hoped, perhaps foolishly, her mother might reach out to console her, but Elisha Wade hadn't even bothered to send flowers or a card to show she cared.

Audie's mind wandered back to the only time her mother had met Carlie.

"Are you sure it'll be fine that I attend your father's funeral with you, darling?" Carlie asked as Audie signaled to pass a tractor-trailer on Interstate-10, heading west.

"You're my wife," Audie said, glancing into the rearview mirror. "Thank you for coming with me."

"You haven't talked much about your dad, and I wish I'd had a chance to meet him while he was still alive. Tell me about him."

"He was a quiet man, unassuming, you know," Audie said and smiled. "Very patient and gentle. He had to be to stay married to my mother. He was a good father who encouraged my brothers and me to make the most out of our lives and live a life that made us happy. He was teaching geology at New Mexico State. Before I was born, he worked for the government."

"Doing what?"

"I don't know. He claimed it was some top-secret project. He quit that job and moved to Las Cruces, where I was born. He enjoyed teaching, then coming home to what he called the simple life," Audie said and laughed. "When I got older, he took me on treks throughout the countryside to look for stuff I thought was interesting. I mostly liked it because he let me dig in the red dirt and piss my mother off by returning home filthy as a pig."

"Sounds like you enjoyed upsetting your mother."

"It was my favorite pastime, and it hasn't changed. I've never failed to be a constant disappointment in my mother's eyes. I'll do everything I can to prevent her from hurting you."

Carlie shifted in the passenger seat and softly rested a hand on Audie's thigh. "You've never disappointed me, love," she said and smiled.

Ten hours later, Audie turned into the semi-circular drive in front of a low-slung adobe home with reddish tile shingles, surrounded by local succulent plants. Audie stepped out of their vehicle and stretched to work out the stiffness in her joints before walking around the car to open the passenger door for Carlie. She took Carlie's hand as they walked slowly up the brick walkway toward the enclosed entry courtyard, where a wooden swing was suspended from the lattice covering.

"It's a lovely home," Carlie said as she glanced at the surroundings. "Very welcoming."

"I guess," Audie muttered. "It hasn't changed much since the last time I was here."

The bright green front door opened, and a tall man stepped outside. His brown eyes passed over Audie and Carlie for a moment before he took a step closer and said, "I'm glad you could make it, Audra."

"It's good to see you, too, Keith," Audie responded coolly. She glanced at Carlie, still tightly gripping her hand. "Honey, this is my brother, Keith. Keith, my wife, Carlie."

Carlie stepped slightly closer and extended her hand. "It's a pleasure to finally meet you, Keith. My condolences for your loss."

"Thank you," Keith said, taking her hand briefly.

"Is Billy here yet?" Audie asked. "Where's Mom?"

"Billy flew in last night, and Mom's holding court in the living room," Keith said. "I just came out to get a breath of fresh air and give my ears a break."

"I'll talk to you later, then," Audie said as she moved toward the front door.

They stepped inside, and Audie placed her hand on the small of Carlie's back to escort her into the front hallway. A woman stepped out of the dining room and smiled when she saw Audie and Carlie.

"Hi," she said pleasantly. "I'm Karen Wade, Keith's wife."

Audie offered her hand. "Audie Wade, Keith's sister. And this is my wife, Carlie."

Karen pulled Audie into a hug and said, "I'm so glad you came, both of you. I'm sure Elisha will be glad to see you, too."

"I doubt that, but we had to come to pay our respects to my father," Audie said.

"Would you take this drink to your mother while Carlie and I put together plates for you both? You must be starving after driving for so long."

Carlie followed Audie's sister-in-law into the dining room where a long table laden with food was located. Audie made her way down the tiled hallway and stood quietly in the archway of the living room. Her mother sat on an overstuffed chair, surrounded by family members and a few others Audie assumed were either friends or university colleagues of her parents. Audie sucked in a deep, calming breath before walking across the large, open room to hand her mother the glass of tea Karen had asked her to deliver. Elisha looked up at her daughter, took the offered glass, and stared at Audie.

"You look well, Audra," Elisha Wade said.

"So do you, Mother," Audie said, leaning down to drop a quick kiss on her mother's cheek.

"Audie!" a loud voice boomed. Audie turned around barely

in time to catch her younger brother before he enveloped her in a tight bear hug, nearly knocking her off her feet.

Audie laughed, returning his exuberance, "You haven't changed a bit," she managed.

"Are you taller or did I shrink?" He laughed.

"I'm the same height, so I guess you shrank," she kidded. "Try standing up straighter," she added, poking him on the arm.

Billy released his sister and quirked an eyebrow when he noticed Carlie. "And who's this?" he asked Audie.

"This is my wife, Carlie," Audie said and smiled. "Honey, my baby brother, Billy Wade." Audie turned slightly toward her mother. "And this is my mother, Dr. Elisha Wade."

Billy didn't hesitate to enclose Carlie in a friendly embrace. "Damn, Audie! I've been married twice, and neither was as good-lookin' as this one. Way to go, Sis," he said and laughed.

Eventually, Carlie set her plate down and approached Elisha. She squatted down in front of the older woman and took her hand between her own.

"My deepest condolences, Dr. Wade," Carlie said.

"Thank you," Elisha replied.

Carlie remained in the background rather than beside Audie during the funeral service.

Audie was sure Carlie and her mother never spoke again after their initial meeting. The thought that her mother hadn't bothered to acknowledge Audie's loss now bothered her.

Once she was finally alone, Audie unplugged the house phone and turned off her cell. She could finish what she needed to do more quickly if she didn't have well-wishers calling every few minutes. It was nice to have acquired so many friends over their years together, but Audie wondered where they had all been when Carlie was wasting away day after month after year.

It was a hard time for Audie, working all day and coming home to care for Carlie every night. It wasn't that Carlie was demanding. She worried all the time that she was interfering with Audie's life. Wasn't that what marriage was all about? In sickness and in health until death....

Of course, no one thinks about the reality of that promise when they make it. A few of their friends drifted away. Audie supposed they found it too depressing to see Carlie as her cancer worsened, despite the chemotherapy and radiation treatments. Once Carlie, who was an amazingly beautiful woman, began losing her hair, as well as weight, she didn't want anyone to see her. Carlie wasn't vain, but she didn't want their friends pretending nothing was wrong when they knew damn well what was happening.

Audie looked at her reflection as she passed the hall mirror. Carlie's illness took a physical toll on her as well, and she noticed a few extra wrinkles that she swore weren't there two weeks ago. But she'd had a surprisingly good night's sleep for the first time in at least a year, and physically she felt oddly relaxed for the first time in...well, a very long time.

The house was quiet, but filled with memories of Carlie and their life together. Audie could still occasionally hear the lilting sound of Carlie's laughter. Before she got so ill and could barely talk, Carlie wrote down a list of things she wanted other people to have. Mostly jewelry or knickknacks she'd accumulated over the years.

For hours Audie sifted through Carlie's things, packing them away and labeling everything. Most of it she knew she wouldn't be able to part with. At least not right away. Maybe later when she adjusted more to Carlie's absence, if she ever did. She left Carlie's office for last.

Most of the paperwork would have to be taken to their accountant. Carlie made arrangements to sell her advertising and promotion company to one of her junior associates. Audie thought she could have sold it for five times the amount Carlie asked for it, but Carlie wanted to let someone she trained buy it with its already established clientele.

Audie opened a box brnd began taking Carlie's paperwork from her desk and file cabinets. Their accountant promised to go over everything and compact it as much as possible for tax purposes. Audie planned to rent a storage unit for most of the paperwork and miscellaneous items that she didn't have a clue about.

As she was closing the box, she remembered the wall safe.

Carlie insisted they get one for their personal papers in case of a fire or natural disaster. Audie laughed at the time since she kept her important papers either at her office or in a safe deposit box at their bank.

She found the card she taped under the center desk drawer with the safe combination on it. She moved a framed picture and turned the combination lock. When it clicked, she pulled the door open and began removing papers from the small safe. She sat at the desk and went through each piece of paper. She smiled at some of it. There were old newspaper clippings of Audie driving down a basketball court for a lay-up, or accompanying Carlie to the few social functions Carlie was able to coerce the more introverted Audie into attending.

Audie unrolled a piece of parchment that contained their Canadian marriage license. They had pictures somewhere, too. Probably in one of Carlie's numerous photo albums.

She remembered standing under a huge tree overlooking the Pacific Ocean waiting for Carlie to join her. She recalled the feel of Carlie's touch as she took Audie's hand and promised to love and cherish her forever. She barely remembered the officiant's voice because her head was so filled with the vision that was Carlie. It was a beautiful day. A perfect day. And Audie felt so lucky that a woman as magnificent as Cara Carlson chose her to share her life with.

Mixed in with the papers Audie found a small package wrapped in tissue paper. She opened it carefully and laughed out loud when she saw what was inside. She picked up a tiny gold-plated key and examined it carefully. She gave it to Carlie not long after they started dating. Audie was twenty and sappier than a Vermont maple. A big, tough jock reduced to a mushy school girl by the effervescent young woman who just turned nineteen. She told Carlie it was the key to her heart and didn't remember when Carlie stopped wearing it continuously. As she held it tightly in her hand, her sadness crept in, and a lump formed in her throat as she fingered the accompanying heart she still wore.

She rewrapped the key, set it aside, and continued going through the contents of the safe.

She found four small locked journals at the bottom of the stack. It took her a couple minutes of fiddling with the locks to pop them open. The journals started years earlier. She glanced through them and saw her life with Carlie unfold in front of her. Carlie wrote about their dates, their fights, the making up, the struggle to get their businesses off the ground, buying and renovating their home. There were entries about the purchase of their retreat on the coast and all the work they had put into it to make it uniquely theirs.

Although she didn't recognize all of the names she saw in the early journals, she guessed they were people Carlie knew through her work. In entries dated nearly five years earlier, the tenor of Carlie's writing changed. Her words were less upbeat and the topics more business oriented and less descriptive. There were hints in the wording that seemed to indicate Carlie was unhappy about something.

July 15, 2014. Things were harried at work today. Wish Audie was home, but she's off on another business trip with Suzanne. The house is too damn quiet. A.L. called again today begging to meet with me, despite my continued disinterest.

August 5, 2014. A.L. actually drove to Austin today and dragged me out to lunch. Audie called and will be away longer than anticipated. I miss her terribly and am considering driving to the coast for the weekend. The fresh air and smell of the sea would do me good.

Chapter Three

Bright and early the next morning, Audie pulled her Subaru Outback onto Interstate-35, which would take her through San Antonio and link up with the highway south to the coast. Buck sat in the back seat with his nose pressed lightly against a crack at the top of the window as he took in the scents of cattle and horses in the fields along the road. Audie lowered the side window slightly so he could pick up other interesting scents as well. She smiled as she watched his nose twitch when he picked up a new scent.

As she cruised through San Antonio sixty minutes later, she noticed traffic was light closer to the coast, but she figured it would likely soon be virtually non-existent. January wasn't exactly the tourist season, but it was their favorite time to go to the beach retreat, because no one would be around to disturb them or drop in for a neighborly visit.

It would be a little past noon before Audie arrived, but that still left her plenty of time before she met with the realtor at three to discuss the possibility of placing the prime beachfront property on Mustang Island up for sale.

Music from her car stereo reminded Audie of the trips she and Carlie made there as they chit-chatted about whatever mindless topics came into their heads or loudly sang along, out of tune, with songs they liked. In the twenty-two years before Carlie's illness, they'd settled into a comfortable life together. They were as different as night and day, except for the little things. If they'd been too much alike, they both thought their lives would have been boring.

Finding even a small seashell would excite Carlie, while Audie would have preferred finding something much larger before she bothered with it. Hanging on their bedroom wall at the retreat was a large, three-dimensional collage of shells, sea glass, and other treasures Carlie collected from the beach over the years.

A little before one that afternoon, Audie lifted a small suitcase from the back of her vehicle and carried it onto the deck entrance of the bungalow while Buck investigated the area and marked his territory around the building. The wind blew briskly off the water, causing Audie to zip up her jacket as she looked out at the choppy whitecaps on the Gulf of Mexico. The only sounds were those of the waves falling on the shoreline and the screeching of the ever-present seagulls.

Audie smiled and recalled how much Carlie loved the smell of the breezes blowing in from the Gulf, the feel of sand between her toes, and the romantic sound of waves drifting through their bedroom window at night. She vividly remembered the nights they spent together there. Their passion for one another was renewed each time they went to the retreat. That special spirit faded a little as their work flourished in Austin. The last few trips Carlie made to the retreat had been alone, with Audie promising to make time to go with her the "next" time. Now Audie wished they could have made one last trip together to this special place—their special place.

****

Audie and Carlie walked leisurely along the shoreline of Mustang Island, enjoying the peace and quiet of the virtually deserted barrier island. The breeze was cool since it was February, but the sun was shining brightly. Audie grasped Carlie's small hand, occasionally pulling her close enough to the water to get their feet wet.

Buck was only a gangly puppy and had to investigate everything. The cold water didn't seem to bother him at all when he waded in to retrieve a piece of driftwood or follow a crab trying to escape his inquisitive nose.

"This is a wonderful time to come to the coast." Carlie smiled as she bent down to investigate another small shell. She rinsed it off and examined it before dropping it in the pocket of Audie's hoodie.

"My pocket is getting full, baby," Audie said and smiled.

"I know," Carlie said, stopping in front of her. "But I love that you don't mind being my personal pack animal." Carlie pushed up on her toes and kissed Audie tenderly. "But not as much as I love the way you touch me."

"Is that an invitation?" Audie grinned, encircling her wife's waist and lifting her into another deep kiss.

"Perhaps," Carlie said against Audie's lips. When Audie lowered her back to the sand, Carlie turned and leaned against Audie as she glanced down the beach. "Where's Buck?"

"Probably following a scent," Audie answered before whistling loudly. A few seconds later, the gangly Retriever bounded over a low hillock and charged toward his owners, jumping enthusiastically into Carlie's arms while Audie braced her body to act as a backstop to prevent Carlie from falling on her ass. "What did you find, buddy?" Audie asked as she vigorously ruffled his head and ears in an affectionate greeting.

Carlie finally dropped him carefully to the sand again. He barked once before trotting back up the low rise above the beach, stopping at the top and barking once more as if calling his humans to follow him. When they reached the top of the rise, Buck shot toward an abandoned-looking structure and wriggled his body through an opening in a sheet of old, weather-beaten plywood that covered what might have been a doorway. Carlie followed Buck and reached out to pull at the floppy plywood.

"Don't do that, baby. The building is leaning and looks like it could collapse," Audie said.

"Help me, Audie," Carlie called out. "I want to see what's inside."

"Probably nothing but a pile of seagull shit," Audie said and approached the hazardous-looking structure.

"Aren't you at least curious? There might be a hidden treasure inside," Carlie said with a mischievous gleam in her eyes.

"Somehow, I seriously doubt that," Audie said and snorted as she grabbed the plywood barrier with both hands. "Stand back in case the whole thing collapses when I jerk on this."

The nails holding the wood in place snapped the second Audie tugged on the plywood and fell away. "Well, that was easy," Audie mumbled. "But I think I picked up a splinter," she added, looking at her hand.

Carlie grabbed Audie's hand, kissed it, and laughed. "I

think you'll survive. Let's check out the inside."

Audie reluctantly followed but needed to duck to get through the doorway. "Just how short were the people that lived here?"

"You could always put in taller doors, sweetie." Carlie shrugged and smiled. She stood in the middle of the large open living area and looked around, taking in everything. Audie could almost see and hear the wheels in Carlie's mind furiously whirling around as she pictured what the old building could be. Carlie swung around and said almost reverently, "It's perfect, darling."

"For what?" Audie asked. "Sheep and goats? It would take a fortune to make it even marginally livable."

"Come on. Let's check out the rest of it." Carlie took Audie's hand and pulled her into the other rooms as she described what she envisioned in her mind.

By the following spring, Audie found herself standing on a tall ladder, tearing down the wet ceiling and checking the rafters of what Carlie was now calling "their retreat." She had already replaced the interior and exterior studs and hoped to install the new roofing tiles during this trip.

Originally, the building was owned by an old guy named Shrimp Steve, who operated a shrimp boat out of Port Aransas. When he passed away, he had no family, and his bungalow sat abandoned for two decades. The realtor Audie contacted suggested the whole building be bulldozed. The original property was considered prime beachfront and was worth a fortune. Considering what it would cost to repair the small house, Audie thought haggling the price down to $25,000 was a victory. She called in a structural engineer to get an opinion and hired an electrician and plumber to bring it up to code.

The remaining manual labor was left to Audie and Carlie. Before each trip to the island, Audie ordered material for what she planned to work on that weekend or vacation. She figured it would take a year to get everything the way she and Carlie wanted it to be.

They usually stayed at a hotel in Port Aransas, but this trip Carlie wanted to stay at the retreat. Carlie packaged foil dinners she could cook on the grill or in a fire on the beach. Audie hooked up an outside shower for them. After dinner, they were both usually too tired to do much except collapse onto their padded palettes and fall asleep.

Audie was sleeping soundly and enjoying a wonderful dream that brought a smile to her lips. She woke and rolled onto her side and slipped her hand over Carlie's hip before skimming it up her wife's abdomen to rest below her breast. She felt hands in her hair and snuggled closer, not waking until soft warm lips covered hers. "I want you, baby," she mumbled.

"I'm right here, lover," Carlie mumbled back as her tongue traced Audie's lips.

Audie pushed her body up and slowly lowered it to cover Carlie's before moving down to suck a nipple deeply into her mouth as her hand slid between Carlie's thighs, searching for the welcoming wetness she knew she'd find. "Oh, baby, I love your touch so much," Carlie said quietly and then moaned as she arched and pressed Audie's mouth more closely against her.

Audie heard thunder in the distance but ignored it until fat, cold raindrops began falling on her bare back. By then she was too engrossed in making love to her wife to stop, rather enjoying the feel of her drenched body slipping over Carlie's. By the time Carlie finally collapsed beneath her and Audie raised her head, both women were soaked, and water ran from Audie's face and hair. They laughed and held one another until the small shower passed.

"I guess tomorrow I should consider getting the roof tiles up." Audie chuckled, shaking water from her head.

****

Audie snapped her fingers and said softly, "Buck." As she looked around the retreat, she was glad to see that it hadn't suffered any damage from the many Gulf storms that tore through there. She pushed open the outside window shutters and the French doors leading into the house and took a deep breath. Buck came in as soon as the door was opened and followed his nose through the front rooms, his toenails tapping on the colorful Mexican floor tiles they'd found in Matamoros.

The inside smelled dank and musty. Buck sneezed, but Audie knew opening the windows would quickly bring freshness into the moderate-sized, two-bedroom bungalow. Audie walked through the rooms and pulled off the sheets that had covered the furniture for the last two years. If she decided to sell the property, she would let the furniture remain with the retreat. There wasn't room for it in their house in Austin, and new owners could replace it if they wanted.

Audie went to her car and retrieved two bags of groceries she'd gotten in Aransas Pass before crossing the causeway to the island. She put the food away and unpacked her bag and sat on the bed for a few moments. When they found the run-down bungalow, they renovated it to suit their tastes, and she couldn't help but wonder what changes new owners might make. Then again, she didn't want to think about it and opened the windows.

Taking a long, slow walk down the beach would give the place time to air out. She snapped her fingers again, and Buck jumped up from the floor. "Time to let your friends know you're back, pal," she said as she thumped the big animal solidly on his side. He pranced in front of her, eager to go outside again.

When she opened the deck doors, Buck flew outside, leaping off the deck and racing to the beach in front of the bungalow, scattering small groups of seagulls. Audie smiled, knowing the ever-present gulls would keep Buck occupied while they were on the coast. Even though he'd never caught one, he always tried like hell.

It was a little after three when Audie heard the sound of gravel crunching under car tires. She was cold after walking along the beach, so she started a fire in the fireplace. She poured a cup of fresh coffee right as there was a knock at the deck doors. Buck barked before escorting Audie to see who was there. Audie was greeted by an attractive, well-tanned, middle-aged blonde.

"Ms. Wade?" the woman asked cheerfully. "I'm Monica Lampley. I believe we spoke on the phone yesterday." She held her hand out, and after sniffing it for a moment, Buck returned to the fireplace to curl up on his usual spot, a padded rug Carlie had made just for him.

Audie stepped aside and said, "Please come in, Mrs. Lampley."

Mrs. Lampley entered the great room and looked around. "This is a beautiful house, Ms. Wade. Very well kept up. Is there any particular reason you might want to part with it?"

"My wife recently passed away, and the house became my sole property through her estate. But I doubt I'll be making many trips down here, so it doesn't really make much sense to keep it."

"I'm very sorry for your loss, Ms. Wade."

"Thank you. Let me show you the rest of the house."

Audie guided Mrs. Lampley through the remaining rooms and waited for her to fill out pages of description for each one.

"No one has been here in nearly two years," Audie explained. "But I hired a man in town to act as caretaker during our…my absence. Everything I've checked so far seems to be in good working order."

"I can tell you that you'd get a tidy sum for this property, if you decided to sell."

An hour later, Mrs. Lampley drove her Cadillac away, leaving Audie with an estimate, her memories, and more packing. This packing job couldn't be any worse than the twenty-four years' worth she'd already done in Austin. Carlie always left a few clothes at the retreat.

There were a few times when Carlie came here by herself to work on a presentation for a potential client or to be alone. Audie didn't mind that she needed solitude sometimes. Everyone did.

She opened the drawers of their dresser and smiled as she touched the familiar intimate garments. Carlie knew exactly what Audie liked, and she could look so incredibly desirable that it took Audie's breath away. Audie picked up a soft silk sleep shirt and buried her face in it. No matter how many times it was washed, it still held Carlie's distinctive scent.

This was much harder than Audie thought it would be. Everything at their retreat seemed intimate and highly personal, meant to be seen by no one other than the two of them. She took a deep breath and slowly released it in an attempt to shake her feelings off as she resumed her packing. She pulled the last piece from the drawer and uncovered a lace handkerchief she didn't recognize. She picked it up and examined it carefully. She'd never seen it before, but it was monogrammed with her initial, A. Maybe Carlie bought it as a present for her and had forgotten it, although it really wasn't something that Audie would ordinarily own or use.

The nightstand on Carlie's side of the bed only held a few things, but Audie was surprised to find another journal. She couldn't believe that Carlie, a committed journal keeper, would have left one at the retreat. Audie shook her head and thumbed through a few pages, laughing at some of the things Carlie had written, saddened by others. In the last half of the journal, Carlie began writing in less detail than the journals Audie had read in Austin. Pulling a pillow behind her, Audie lay back to read Carlie's thoughts, resting an arm on Buck's back and running her fingers through his thick fur.

September 2017: The weather along the coast has been terrible. We have been cooped up inside the bungalow for two or three days, mostly talking and consuming un-Godly amounts of coffee and wine. Although it hasn't been all bad, a time to become better acquainted. It has been nearly three months, and I must admit that I have been looking forward to this time we have together. Everything about her is so very interesting. Plus, there is the risk involved with agreeing to meet her here. I'm not exactly sure why I am.

Her? Audie thought. *What risk?* After all the years they were together, she couldn't think of anything they didn't already know about each other. The date was only three years earlier, but Audie couldn't remember the last time they went to the retreat together.

October 2017: What an incredible weekend! I would not have believed how much more alive I am feeling now than I was when I came here before. God forgive me for hiding what I have been feeling. It seems so very unfair to Audie, and yet she always makes my homecoming incredibly sweet. My times here have made my most intimate moments with Audie even more open and intense. But I don't know how to tell her the truth yet. I've hidden it for so long.

November 2017: I find that I am actually looking forward

to these times. I never envisioned A.L.'s understanding and forgiveness. I wish I could explain it. The life I have with Audie is safe and secure, and I love her with all that I am. But to lose the peacefulness these times have brought into my life...I don't know that I'm willing to give it up now even if I wanted to.

The last entry had been made a little over two years ago, shortly after Carlie was diagnosed with breast cancer.

December 2017: This will be my last visit to our retreat, and the thought of that saddens me more than mere words can express, but I had to see her one final time. She asks nothing of me, demands nothing, and yet I know I owe her an explanation. She has brought so much joy into my life in such a short period of time. How she will take the end of something that is ending before either of us are ready I cannot guess. I am filled with sadness and regret for the loss of our special and fulfilling relationship. I hope someday she will understand my choices and be able to forgive me.

As Audie started to close the journal, not believing what the entries had implied, she saw a piece of paper peeking from the back. It was actually a photograph, and at a glance it looked like it had been taken on the beach near the retreat. Audie almost couldn't register what she was seeing. It was Carlie, but she wasn't alone. A beautiful young blonde had her arms wrapped around Carlie's shoulders, and Carlie's hands covered the blonde's hands. Both were smiling broadly. Audie didn't know when the picture was taken. She hadn't taken it and didn't recognize the woman with Carlie. She turned the picture over and saw Carlie's distinctive handwriting: *August 2017.*

****

Late the next evening, Audie waited impatiently for the front door to open. Shoving her hands into the pockets of her down jacket, she prowled the small enclosed porch. When the door finally opened, her brother-in-law smiled at her.

"Audie! Good to see you. Get on in here and warm up, girl."

"Thanks, Jerry," Audie said as she stepped past him. "Lynn home?"

"In the kitchen. Go on back."

Audie unzipped her jacket and strode down the hall toward the kitchen, the aroma of homemade chicken noodle soup greeting her nose. Lynn smiled when she saw Audie enter the country-style kitchen.

"Hey, Audie. Coffee?" Lynn asked as she stirred a large pot.

"No, thanks. I have to talk to you, Lynn," Audie said, agitated.

Lynn reached down and turned off the eye under the pot. She placed her hand on Audie's arm. "Is something wrong, hon?"

Audie reached into her jacket, took out the picture, and tossed it on the kitchen counter. "You tell me, Lynn. Who the hell is this?"

Lynn picked up the photo and glanced at it briefly before laying it back down. "Where did you get that?"

"It was in one of Carlie's journals at the retreat. Who the hell is that woman?" Audie demanded, pointing at the picture.

"I think maybe something stronger than coffee might be needed," Lynn said as she turned away from Audie.

Audie grabbed Lynn's arm and stopped her. "Was Carlie having an...affair?" she demanded, her voice cracking.

When Lynn looked at Audie's hand, Audie released her. Lynn opened a cabinet and took down a bottle of Chivas and two glasses. She carefully poured the rich alcohol into the glasses then pointed to the kitchen table. "Sit down, Audie. Please." Lynn crossed to the refrigerator and dropped two ice cubes in each glass. She placed one in front of Audie. Lynn took a slow drink before speaking.

"Her name is Amanda Lange," Lynn said quietly.

Audie felt her blood run cold and her face harden as she threw the drink down her throat and slammed the glass down on the table. "Tell me, Lynn."

"Carlie loved you very much, Audie. You don't really

want to know…"

"Yes, Lynn. I *do* want to know. Was Carlie having a fucking affair?"

"It wasn't what you think."

"You have no idea what I'm thinking! How long was she cheating on me?"

"I don't really…"

"I know you know, Lynn. Carlie told you everything!" Audie seethed.

"Carlie and Amanda only knew one another for…a while."

When Audie stood up, her six-foot-two frame towered over Lynn. "How long?" she demanded again, louder this time.

"Until Carlie got sick," Lynn said flatly. "Carlie never saw her again. She didn't want to hurt her."

"Let me get this straight," Audie said as she began to pace. "For four fucking years while I was away, working, my wife, the woman I loved unconditionally, and was faithful to, for over twenty years, was fucking this…Amanda person. And when I returned home, she pretended nothing had changed and fucked me, too. That about right?"

"She loved you so much, Audie."

"And where was this woman while Carlie was dying?"

"Audie, I…"

"Where is Amanda Lange now?"

"I have no idea. I've never actually met her. Carlie met her on the coast. That's all I know."

Audie sat down heavily then looked at Lynn, tears pooling in her eyes. "Why would she do it, Lynn? I gave her everything. I don't understand."

"She told me once that meeting Amanda changed her life."

"Great! So her life with me wasn't enough?"

Covering Audie's hand with her own, Lynn smiled slightly. "She never stopped loving you or loved you less. Amanda was just…well, special. Carlie told me that in some strange way meeting Amanda lifted a burden off her shoulders and allowed her to feel freer when she was with you."

Audie wiped her eyes and laughed slightly. "That's bullshit and you know it, Lynn. And just this afternoon I was feeling guilty."

"Oh, my God! Did *you* have an affair?"

"No, I wasn't having an affair. Carlie was the only woman in my life since the day we met. But about six months ago, before she died, I picked up a total stranger that I didn't give a shit about, and I fucked her. It was just fuckin', okay, but sure as shit wasn't love. Carlie's illness and work and everything else was crushing me, and I needed to feel physically wanted for just a little while. At the most it was stress management, and it only happened that once. No one was hurt by it."

"I'm sorry, Audie. I didn't know Carlie kept anything that might lead you to Amanda."

"Does she even know that Carlie died?"

"I doubt it. I wouldn't know how to contact her. Carlie told me she decided not to see her again after she was diagnosed."

"But obviously she never forgot her."

Chapter Four

One year later

Audie leaned back in her office chair and took a swallow of her tenth cup of cold coffee for the day. Last year she cleaned out everything in her office that reminded her of Carlie. Now there were no pictures, no knickknacks, and finally, there was no scent to bring her memories back to life.

She often thought about Carlie and was glad she was able to make her last days comfortable, but the idea of Carlie cheating still haunted her. She was interrupted by a tap at her door, followed by Suzanne, her business partner, strolling into her office. Suzanne Travers had been Audie's best friend and mentor for almost twenty years and her coach in the final year of her collegiate basketball career. The day after Audie received her law degree, Suzanne called her, asking her to become the legal part of her new business managing and representing female athletes with promising careers ahead of them. Now, after eight years, they had a solid business.

"What's up?" Audie asked.

"I've been thinking we should organize a get-together between our clients and some of the WNBA folks. There've been quite a few calls lately."

"Already booked."

"Good," Suzanne said as she poured a cup of coffee for herself. "You've always been more organized than I am. Damn good thing."

"I've got a company putting together some highlight reels for some of the girls who didn't receive as much television coverage as the others. And I've hired a diction coach for a few of them who sound a little more like Scarlett O'Hara than I'd like."

"Good idea," Suzanne said. "So, I've been thinking lately."

"I'm happy to hear that you've finally decided to try that for a change." Audie smiled and took another sip of her coffee.

"Smart ass," Suzanne mumbled. "Anyway, I think you should start getting out more often."

"I don't know, Suzanne." Audie paused. "It wouldn't be the same."

"Maybe not, but you could start with something simple."

"I'm not ready to have people at my house again," Audie said and frowned. "Carlie always handled our social engagements."

"Gia and I are going to an art exhibit this weekend, and I think it would be a great way for you to ease back into the local social scene. How about it?"

"Really?" Audie said with a look of distaste. "That was more Carlie's thing than mine."

"True, but maybe if you're there, you can save me a small fortune. Gia's interested in some new artist she's heard about, and that always means *mucho dinero* for me."

"It'll probably cost you either way." Audie laughed.

"I know," Suzanne said with a grin. "But she still thinks I'm pretty cute and will forgive me after a couple of earnest kisses. Hey! That's what you could use, too."

"What?"

"A little kissing, earnest or not."

"Not interested, Suzanne," Audie said and frowned. "Drop it."

"Okay. Then how about grabbing your gym clothes and playing a little one-on-one. We can work off some frustration. And you can use it. You're getting a little flabby around the middle, my friend."

"I weigh exactly the same as I did when we met," Audie sneered.

"But it's shifted, so get your shit, and I'll kick your ass, just like I did when I was your coach and you thought you were hot shit," Suzanne said and stuck her hand out. "And if I win, you'll agree to go to that art show with us."

"That'll be the day."

****

"You realize, of course, that I don't want to do this." Audie frowned as she tied her sneaker laces tightly.

"Tough," Suzanne said, tossing the basketball across the court. "Just dribble the damn ball. It's like riding a bicycle or making love. With a little practice, it'll come back to you."

"I know how to play fuckin' basketball," Audie snapped. "I have a million things to get done back at the office."

"Don't worry, the paperwork fairy isn't likely to make an appearance any time soon. It'll still be there in an hour or two." Suzanne tightened the drawstring on her lightweight sweatpants as she walked toward Audie.

Audie flipped the ball over in her hands and looked at Suzanne. "We don't have to do this, Suzanne. I'm fine, really."

"You're out of shape, and we both know it. Hell, woman, you haven't done anything physically productive since Carlie died. If this is the only way I can get your ass out somewhere—"

"I don't need to go out, damn it. I'm fine," Audie snapped as she began to dribble the ball in place. She didn't have time for this crap.

Suzanne slapped the ball from Audie's hand, stole it, and made her way to the basket for an easy lay-up. After she tossed the ball back to Audie, she said, "That's one point for me. Come on, Audie! Where's that annoying competitive spirit? It's like you died along with Carlie."

"Can we not talk about this right now?" Audie groused.

Suzanne approached Audie and spread her arms in a defensive position. "Would you rather I made an appointment?"

Audie turned slightly and looked over her shoulder toward the basket. "I'd rather we never talked about it at all, old lady."

"Whatever." Suzanne shrugged then placed a hand on Audie's hip, keeping her body between Audie and the basket. "Now show me what you got, if anything, ya pussy."

Audie laughed and continued to dribble while lowering her six-two frame slightly. The ball felt familiar and comfortable as it met her hand over and over. There were a dozen different ways she knew she could take the ball to the rim, and for a few moments she allowed her mind to scan through the possibilities.

Twenty-five years earlier she hadn't even had to think about it. Her body did it all so automatically and effortlessly. Right up until the night that big dyke from Missouri landed on her knee and ended a promising future. Audie healed, but by the beginning of the next season it became obvious she would never be the player she once was. There were a few spectators who thought the Missouri girl did it on purpose to put Audie out of commission, if only temporarily. But who knew? Coulda just been one of those things.

Twenty years ago, she wouldn't have believed Carlie could ever be unfaithful as she held Audie's hand in the ambulance on the way to the hospital emergency room. But Audie was injured, and Carlie was unfaithful. Coulda just been another one of those things.

"Come on, ya lard ass!" Suzanne hissed. "Do something, for God's sake, before I die of old age."

Feigning a lean to her right, Audie switched the ball quickly to her left hand and spun around Suzanne, driving from the top of the key to the basket before Suzanne could recover from her own lean to the right. One bounce and up…nothing but net.

"That what you had in mind?" Audie smirked.

"Took you long enough." Suzanne smiled, grabbing the ball and returning to mid-court.

Twenty minutes later, they took a water break. As Audie leaned back against the folded bleachers in the small gym, she took a long drink of water and wiped her forehead with a small towel. "You were right, Suzanne. It does feel good to kick your ass again." She grinned and took another sip of water.

"Well, since I got five years on you, I can't say I'm too impressed."

"That's just too much of Gia's exotic Italian cuisine talkin'."

"We need to start going to the gym and working out again."

"Probably right. I feel a little sluggish."

The end door of the gym popped open, and two women entered. As Suzanne and Audie watched, the younger women shot a few baskets and ran around warming up. One of them had curly dark blonde hair streaked with light blonde highlights and pulled back into a ponytail. Her companion had incredibly short, spiky, dark hair.

Ponytail stripped off a lightweight jacket and adjusted her hair. She wore a faded UT T-shirt over bright orange shorts. Audie scanned the long, tan legs under the orange shorts and appreciated the muscle definition. The taller brunette wore a white T-shirt over baggy, gray thinclads. The two women laughed and pushed at each other as they went through a game of horse, shooting from various places on the court.

"What do you think?" Suzanne said and took another drink.

"About what?" Audie asked absently.

"Think we could take them?"

Audie estimated them to be in their late twenties or early thirties. Both looked physically fit. The dark-haired woman was obviously the stronger of the two. She was well built with broad, muscular shoulders. To Audie she looked more like a linebacker than a basketball player, but she was a good shooter. The blonde was slightly shorter and weighed less but was deceptively quick on her feet.

"Probably," Audie said as she looked over at Suzanne. "You take blondie, and I'll take the butch."

"You think I can't handle her?"

"I'm sure you can, but you'd have to explain the bruises to Gia later."

"True."

Suzanne pushed her body up from the bleacher seat, stepped down, and walked toward the two laughing women. She spoke to them for a few minutes, nodded, and trotted back. "They said they only have about a half hour, but I'll probably be half dead by then anyway," Suzanne said as she rested a foot on the bleacher to tighten the laces on her sneakers.

Audie stood slowly, stretched her arms over her head, and swiveled her waist to loosen up. "Just don't bitch later. It was your bright idea to get some exercise anyway. I was perfectly happy sitting behind my desk going over those contracts you wanted yesterday. But, noooo, you just felt the need to sweat and strain your muscles."

"Quit bitchin'. Just for you, I'll extend the deadline for those contracts until day after tomorrow."

"Thanks a heap," Audie grumbled as they ambled across the court toward the younger women. Pointing at the brunette, she said, "Y'all can be on offense first."

Nodding, the woman dribbled to the half court, while the blonde smiled brightly and joined Suzanne near the two-point line and waited. The brunette passed the ball to the blonde, who immediately tried to run past Suzanne. For a fifty-year-old woman, Suzanne was surprisingly nimble and kept close to the woman to cut off her angle to the basket. As Audie stood with her arms spread, the brunette's back against her, she waited for a pass to come.

As soon as the ball was in her hands, the woman swung around, jabbing her elbow into Audie's abdomen a little harder than Audie believed necessary, but she didn't say anything about it. Taking two steps forward and one back, the woman fired off a shot toward the basket; the ball ran around the rim before finally falling in. As the two younger women high-fived, Suzanne picked up the ball and returned to half court.

Audie glared at the brunette for a moment. So that's the way it's going to be, she thought.

Even though she hadn't wanted to play, Audie's competitive nature simply would not allow her to do anything other than play aggressively. When she looked at Suzanne, resting her hands on her thighs, she saw her friend smiling at her. Suzanne knew Audie much too well to know she wouldn't take the rough play lying down.

Suzanne tossed the ball to Audie. In a play she felt confidant would work, Audie drove to the basket and passed the ball off to Suzanne at the last second, allowing her an easy lay-up.

The game went on for nearly half an hour longer with the brunette "accidentally" hitting Audie two more times. The score of the pick-up game was tied, and all four players were getting tired. The brunette tossed the ball to the blonde and went immediately to the basket, waiting for the pass back to her. As she drove forward, Audie stood squarely in the lane, establishing her position. But the woman didn't hesitate and ran into Audie to lift the ball toward the basket. Even though she wasn't knocked down by the blatant charge, Audie still managed to jump into the air and stretch her arm up to deflect the ball off court with her fingertips.

As the woman shook her head and started to retrieve the ball, Audie grabbed her arm and pulled her closer. "That wasn't necessary."

"You'll recover," the woman said, jerking her arm away.

Leaning closer, Audie said in a low voice, "Do it again and I'll rip your fuckin' head off."

"Are you threatening me?" The woman stepped closer into Audie's space, bumping her chest against Audie's.

"You're damn right I am!"

"If you can't handle it, get off the fuckin' court, grandma," the woman said and shoved Audie.

Before Suzanne and the blonde could rush over to separate their friends, Audie had shoved the woman against the pads along the wall beneath the net, glaring at her with her hands clinched.

"That's enough, Tracey!" the blonde said loudly. "Jesus Christ, it's just a fuckin' game."

Tracey straightened her shirt and glared at Audie. "Yeah, well, apparently some people can't handle a little competition."

Suzanne reached out and grabbed Audie's arm as she started toward the younger woman again. "It's over, Audie. Time to get back to work."

When the younger women turned to leave, the blonde held onto her companion's shirt to pull her away.

Audie bent over and picked up the basketball. "Hey!" she yelled. When the brunette turned, Audie rocketed the ball toward her, barely allowing her time to reach out and block it. "You forgot your ball."

A moment after blocking the basketball aimed at her head, the brunette broke her friend's grip on her T-shirt and started toward Audie and Suzanne. Audie turned to face the brunette, her fists clenched. Suzanne grabbed Audie's arm, and the blonde grabbed her friend's T-shirt with both hands before blows could be exchanged.

"That was stupid, Audie," Suzanne said as she shoved Audie toward the showers before returning to work.

"Yeah, I know, but that little bitch already got in two or three pretty good hits. Probably have a bruise on my ribcage by tomorrow."

"I'll try to pick someone older and less athletic next time," Suzanne quipped.

****

On Saturday evening, Audie checked her appearance in the full-length mirror in her bedroom. She walked into the adjoining bathroom and spritzed herself with her favorite cologne. Actually, it was Carlie's favorite scent on Audie and usually led to an unforgettably romantic encounter later in the evening. Audie wasn't sure why she still used it. Even knowing that Carlie had betrayed her didn't erase the memories of their time together. The tailored charcoal suit she chose to wear to the art exhibit was a gift from Carlie. It fit perfectly and was cut to show off her tapered waist and broad shoulders. Audie chose a soft, black turtleneck to wear under the suit jacket and small, gold hoop earrings and a diamond tennis bracelet as her only jewelry.

She checked her short black hair and finger combed the longer bangs that swept rakishly across her forehead. A sprinkling of gray began near her temples. There wasn't much she could do about that, though the gray made her look more distinguished.

The art exhibit was being displayed at a gallery adjacent to the warehouse district, and it took Audie a few extra minutes to locate the correct building. She wandered inside the large gallery and removed her coat, dropping it off at a coat check before heading into the exhibition. Apparently, the works of several new artists had been combined to create a group of works by members of a local artists' co-op. Although admittedly not an art aficionado, Audie saw a few pieces she was drawn to and paused to examine them more closely. Carlie called the art Audie occasionally dragged home eclectic, but they suited her tastes.

She stopped to check out an abstract nude created by assorted running drips of bright primary colors of paint. As she stood in front of the painting, she spotted Suzanne and Gia conversing with a young woman. Audie assumed she was one of the artists exhibiting their work. The presumed artist was taller than average and slender. Her curly dark blonde hair was highlighted by lighter blonde streaks. A smattering of glitter sprinkled in her hair sparkled under the overhead lighting. As Audie came closer, she noticed that her vibrant, blue-gray eyes twinkled when she smiled.

Her mid-calf silver dress, highlighted by a fringe of miniature pearls, seemed to reflect everything around her. The woman's eyes quickly scanned Audie as she approached before returning her attention to the person speaking to her.

Gia was dressed in her usual high fashion style, and Suzanne, always impeccably clothed, listened to her wife's conversation while nursing a complimentary glass of wine.

Audie stopped beside them and patted Suzanne on the back, then leaned closer and whispered, "Bored?"

"You know it," Suzanne whispered back. "Not to mention hungry."

"You're always hungry," Audie said and chuckled.

"Oh, Audra," Gia said, grabbing Audie's arm. "Come look at a sculpture with me. It will look magnificent in our backyard garden," she said excitedly as Audie followed her to a display.

The piece Audie found herself staring at was a fountain with water falling from leaf to leaf until it reached a small pool at the bottom. The water flowed continuously, and Audie assumed the water from the pool was being recycled to the leaves via some unseen mechanism. The leaves were smoothly painted with metallic green and yellow auto paint, which should withstand poor weather as well as the persistent heat and bright sunlight of Texas.

"So, what do you think, Audra?" Gia asked.

"It's nice," Audie said and studied the sculpture once more. "Where are you planning to put it? Your backyard is getting a little full."

"My Suzanna will make a place for it. Perhaps you will help her, yes?"

"Well, I don't—" Audie started.

"Come, come, let me introduce you to the artist," Gia insisted, inserting her hand in the crook of Audie's arm to be escorted back to her small party. "You look quite...continental tonight, Audra."

"Thanks, Gia. So do you, as always."

Gia released Audie's arm when they reached Suzanne and curled it around her wife's waist.

"What do you think, Audie?" Suzanne asked.

"I think we're going to be digging a pretty big hole in your backyard very soon," Audie said and smiled. "But personally, I think it might look better in the entry atrium."

"Audra, this is the artist, Reagan Malloy. Reagan, Audra Wade, my Suzanna's business partner," Gia said.

Audie extended her hand and smiled. "Audie, please. Only Gia and my mother call me Audra and usually because they're annoyed with me."

"Did you see anything you might be interested in, Audie?" Reagan asked with a smile that was reflected in her eyes. She took Audie's hand warmly and held it in hers for a moment longer than Audie thought necessary.

"Yes. One, in particular, caught my attention, but I'll have to think about it for a while," Audie said, withdrawing her hand and feeling it cool immediately.

"Audie's tastes are eclectic," Suzanne said. "She doesn't really have just one style."

"That's very interesting." Reagan smiled brightly. "Eclectic art connoisseurs aren't afraid to consider new things. I like that."

"Gia and I have invited Miss Malloy to join us for dinner. Audie, why don't you join us?" Suzanne asked with a smile.

"I was planning to work on those contracts you wanted," Audie said.

"You have all day tomorrow. Plus I extended the deadline, remember? We'll get you home early. I promise."

Reagan reached out and touched Audie's forearm. An arc of static electricity jumped from Reagan's fingers and lightly shocked Audie's arm. "Yes," Reagan said softly, her eyes meeting Audie's. "Please join us. I'd like to learn more about your eclectic taste in art."

****

Audie held out a chair for Reagan after they were escorted to their table before taking her own seat. She opened and glanced at the menu selections. She was a little hungry but didn't want to overeat this close to going to bed.

"What would you recommend?" Reagan asked as she leaned closer to Audie.

"Depends on what you're hungry for," Audie said.

"A burger and fries sound heavenly right now," Reagan said and smiled.

Audie chuckled and said, "I agree, but Gia wouldn't be caught dead in a burger joint. The chopped steak with gravy, mushrooms, and home fries is probably the closest you'll get here. It's not too heavy and not bad with the house salad."

"I gather you prefer simple food then," Reagan said with a smile.

"Nothin' beats a loaded chilidog and a cold beer."

"A woman after my own heart," Reagan said and chuckled. "A cheap date."

"Good to know." Audie grinned as she set the menu on the table.

Reagan ordered the chopped steak, as did Audie. After they ate Suzanne ordered brandy for everyone. Audie sniffed the smoky liquid before taking her first drink.

"All we need now is a smooth, mellow Cuban," Suzanne said.

"Not until we get home, *il mio amore*," Gia said, gazing at Suzanne affectionately. "But then only outside."

Suzanne smiled and took Gia's hand. "I've been thinking lately."

"Still working on that, are you?" Audie asked.

"Sometimes, you just have to, no matter how much it hurts." Suzanne grinned as she shook a finger at Audie. "I think we should start our monthly bull sessions again. We'll even host the first one at our place."

"What are monthly bull sessions?" Reagan asked.

"It's just a gathering of a bunch of friends. We usually start out shooting a little pool or playing terrible poker, but after a few drinks it eventually disintegrates into just shooting the bull about various topics," Suzanne explained.

"Sounds interesting." Reagan smiled.

"What she's not telling you is it usually degenerates into a bunch of middle-aged women bitching about the good old days when they were young and frisky, the search for love, and the general lack of orgasms." Audie smirked.

"We will do it anyway," Gia said calmly. "If you do not wish to rejoin the human race again, that is up to you, Audra."

"That's very European of you, Gianna," Audie replied, with a hint of sarcasm in her tone.

"Speaking of degenerating," Suzanne said quickly, "I now think it's officially past my bedtime."

"This has been a fascinating discussion," Reagan said, pushing her chair back. "Thank you for inviting me this evening."

"It was our pleasure, *mio caro*," Gia said as Suzanne helped her slip into her coat. "We will do it again sometime."

As Gia and Reagan began walking away, Suzanne turned to Audie. "So, what's with you, Audie? You seemed to be having a good time, and then it all went to hell."

"I'm sorry, Suzanne. I just don't think I'm ready to jump back into life the way it used to be. Considering that it wasn't what I thought it was after all."

"You've got to put that business about Carlie behind you. It was only a fluke that you even discovered her supposed affair anyway."

"Did you and Gia know about it? And please don't lie to protect me. It couldn't possibly hurt any more than it already does."

Suzanne took Audie by the shoulders and looked her directly in the eyes. "I swear to you, my very good friend, that *I* did not know. But I suspect that Gia might have, even though I haven't asked her, and she's never spoken about it to me."

"Hey, who was that private investigator you hired a few years ago to do some background checks for you? I want her to locate Amanda Lange for me."

"Then you'll get over it and move on?"

"Possibly," Audie said and shrugged. "Depends on what she finds out."

"I'll give you her card at work Monday, okay?"

Audie and Suzanne joined Gia and Reagan in front of the restaurant. Gia had already sent the valet off to find their Lexus.

"I have told Reagan that we will drive her home," Gia said as Suzanne joined her.

"I can have them call a cab," Reagan said. "I don't want to take you out of your way."

"It's no problem," Suzanne said and smiled. "Where do you live?"

"In North Austin, off the loop. It's a little out of the way."

"I go that way to get home anyway, Suzanne," Audie said. "Why don't I drop her off for you?"

"You sure?" Suzanne asked.

Audie nodded. "If Reagan doesn't object to riding in my lowly Subaru instead of your fancy Lexus."

"Not at all." Reagan smiled.

Five minutes later, Suzanne pulled her Lexus away from the curb as the valet opened the passenger door of Audie's Subaru for Reagan.

"I appreciate the ride," Reagan said and buckled her seatbelt.

"My pleasure," Audie said as she glanced back to check oncoming traffic.

"So, did you actually enjoy my art or were you just being polite?" Reagan asked as Audie accelerated onto the highway.

"Gia would say that I'm never just polite, but I did find it interesting and rather ingenious. However, I'm afraid sculpture has never been my thing. That was more Carlie's area."

"Carlie?"

"My wife. She died about eighteen months ago," Audie said as she changed lanes.

"I'm sorry," Reagan said softly, crossing her legs.

Audie couldn't help but notice the expanse of smooth skin now showing above Reagan's knees. "Yeah, me too."

"So, what kind of lawyer are you?"

"A decent enough one, I think."

Reagan laughed. "That wasn't what I meant," she said as she reached over and lightly punched Audie's arm.

"I know. Mostly I write and negotiate contracts for Suzanne's clients and represent clients who are unhappy with the contracts they've already signed before they come to us," Audie explained succinctly.

"Wow! You do know that most of that zoomed right over my head, right?" Reagan laughed.

"Suzanne represents women who have potentially lucrative

sports futures. She acts as their agent to get them the best monetary deals possible based on their skill level and the demand for those skills. I assure that their eventual contracts reflect that," Audie said as she glanced at Reagan. "Better?"

"You talk like a lawyer," Reagan said with a smile.

"Is that a good thing or a bad thing?"

"I haven't decided yet."

"I hope you'll let me know when you make a decision."

"Was that a sneaky way of asking me out?"

"No. I mean if you…this conversation seems to be straying into unexpected areas, so now who's talking like a lawyer?"

Reagan placed her hand on Audie's thigh and patted it. "I was only kidding you. Just trying to lighten the conversation."

Audie could have continued the bantering with Reagan but didn't. The young woman was charming and attractive, not to mention young. Very young. The thought of her age depressed Audie slightly. She was only forty-five. When had she come to see that as being too old to enjoy her life? Perhaps after Carlie became sick, or after she died when she should have had many more years left. Or perhaps after Audie discovered Carlie's affair with a younger woman.

"Does Suzanne only represent female athletes?" Reagan asked, breaking into Audie's thoughts.

"Pretty much. When I met Suzanne, she was coaching, and many of the girls who played for her wound up playing for regional, semi-professional sports franchises that seemed to be based on the idea that female athletes weren't worth as much as male athletes. Eventually, Suzanne left coaching to represent women in sports and I joined her. It wasn't just the playing contracts she was interested in. It was also the endorsement possibilities. There's probably more money there than in the actual sport. We just want to ensure that women get a fair piece of the action."

"Sounds like a worthwhile cause."

"It can be, even though some of our clients fight with us about what they should do."

"What do you mean?"

"Most of the women we represent come from low economic backgrounds. They only see the money aspect in the short term. What can I buy now that I always wanted but couldn't afford kind of thing. We insist that they sock away a certain percentage and keep it in a holding account for the future. Just like men, it would only take one serious injury to lose it all. Then they'd be right back at the same economic level they started at. Sports are wonderful, but very few of them offer an earning life of more than five or six years, unless you're an exceptional player. Then they still have the rest of their lives to worry about."

"Guess I'd never thought about it that way before."

"The future can sneak up on you faster than you'd think, as you probably gathered from our conversation at dinner. We just want to give them a fighting chance to be comfortable after the fans have found someone newer and younger to cheer for."

"Do you ever represent artists?"

"We've never been approached about it. If you're a successful artist, then you will probably have a career that will span much longer than five or six years."

"But if you're a new artist and just becoming noticed, the contract aspect could be just as important. Although there hopefully aren't many, there are galleries out there that demand more than fifty percent commission for any art they sell."

"That's something your agent or representative should look into." Audie looked at Reagan and smiled.

"I know artists who do it because they love it and say that the money is unimportant as long as people see their art. But personally, even though art is to be appreciated, I don't know anyone who can live on appreciation alone. Take the next exit."

Audie exited the loop and followed the access road.

"You don't remember me, do you?" Reagan asked, taking their conversation in a totally different direction.

"Should I?" Audie asked, glancing at Reagan curiously.

"I should have my feelings hurt, but I look a little different tonight than the first time we met," Reagan said, pretending to pout. "I'm sure you remember my friend Tracey better since she hit you in the ribs pretty hard a few times."

"I still have the bruises to prove it." Audie nodded. "So that was you Suzanne was guarding? Damn! You're quick.

Sorry I didn't recognize you, but you do look a little more sophisticated tonight."

"I recognized you the minute you walked into the exhibition tonight. The way you carry yourself exudes confidence, which shows me you won't let anyone push you around. I like that."

"Obviously, I'm not very observant though. I usually remember attractive women. My apologies. Sometimes I let my competitive nature take over and block out everything around me."

"So does Tracey, otherwise she never would have behaved the way she did that day. I apologize for her."

"I'm sorry if I offended your girlfriend."

"I'm not making excuses, but Tracey isn't my girlfriend. Just a friend. Actually, our mutual friend, Emily, killed herself a couple of years ago, and we're both still a little touchy about it."

"I'm sorry," Audie said, taking Reagan's hand briefly.

Audie followed Reagan's directions until she finally turned into the drive of a small, secluded house on a dead-end street. She hadn't been paying rapt attention to the directions and hoped she would be able to backtrack her way to the loop.

Reagan must have been a mind reader. As she opened the car door she said, "If you go back to the corner and turn left, that road will take you back to the highway in about another mile. Thanks for the lift."

Before Audie could say anything else, Reagan was out of the car and going up the hedged walkway to her front door. Audie watched her move toward the porch and had to admit she enjoyed the view as she waited until she knew that Reagan had opened the front door to her house. It was an old habit she'd heard her mother say a hundred times: "Wait until the person is in their house. You never know who could be lurking in the bushes." It seemed like a ridiculous idea that anyone would hang around all night waiting for someone to come home so they could attack them. But it did seem like the polite thing to do.

In less than ten minutes Audie was back on the highway and gratefully headed home. The wine and brandy had relaxed her initially, but now they were just making her sleepy. Reagan was an interesting young woman. Interesting? Interesting wasn't the right word. Intriguing perhaps. Stunning? Flirtatious? Sensuous? Desirable? All applied to the young artist as well. Audie shook her head and laughed out loud. How about too fucking young? It'd been a long time since Audie thought about being with another woman, but even she wasn't ready to admit that she was desperate enough to rob the cradle.

****

When Reagan entered her house, the first thing she did was go into her bedroom and kick off her shoes. Given the chance, she would never wear shoes, but the showing that night demanded it. As she strolled back toward the kitchen for a glass of water, she couldn't help but think about Audie Wade. What a delightfully interesting woman. There was a quiet intenseness about her that Reagan found dangerously alluring.

Since moving to Austin six months earlier, Reagan had been busy establishing herself with local galleries and artists' groups, and she hadn't taken much time to explore the social scene she had heard so much about—until she saw Audie at the pick-up game she and Tracey played against her and Suzanne. Before then she hadn't seen another woman who even vaguely interested her.

There was something alluring about Audie's confidence and competitiveness that fascinated Reagan. Despite the difference in their ages, Reagan wanted to know Audie Wade better. Audie, with her sweaty body and hair, was definitely interesting, but the cool, calm, collected woman she'd just spent an enjoyable evening with fascinated her. The two sides of Audie Wade beguiled Reagan.

As she crossed the living room and then returned to her bedroom, she turned her cell phone back on and discovered she had two unanswered calls, accompanied by two voice mails. After she pressed a button on her phone, she only heard a second of static when she listened to the first voice message, but she was greeted by a familiar voice on the second message asking her to call whenever she got home. As she plopped down on the couch, she hit the speed dial, and three rings later she heard Tracey's voice on the other end.

"Sorry it's so late, Trace," Reagan said as she stifled a yawn. "I just got in."

"Pretty late for a show, isn't it?"

"I was invited to dinner afterward by a potential buyer, and I never turn down a good meal, especially when it's free," Reagan said and laughed. "So, what's up?"

"Not much. Just checkin' in before I head to bed. How was your exhibit? Sell anything?"

"I did and you'll never guess in a million years who I had dinner with."

"Tell me."

"You remember those two women we had that pick-up game with a couple of weeks ago?" Reagan asked with a smile.

"Remind me," Tracey said.

"They were older. The one guarding you was tall and got a little upset after you elbowed her a few times," Reagan said, trying to think of more details to prod Tracy's memory.

"Oh yeah. I remember now. My elbow was the only way I could keep her off me." Tracey chuckled.

"It mostly pissed her off, I think." Reagan laughed.

"That's who you had dinner with?"

"Yep, but they didn't recognize me until I told the one you elbowed that we'd met before. The tall one, Audie Wade, drove me home after dinner. I liked them both. Very friendly and outgoing. Well, Audie's not that outgoing, but she's still interesting to talk to. Apparently, they've been friends for years and are now business partners."

"You'll have to tell me more next time I see you. How about a burger some night this week?"

"Only if it includes fries and a real old-fashioned shake," Reagan said with a smile.

"Is there any other way?" Tracey laughed.

"You're the best, Trace. Sleep well," Reagan said softly.

"You, too, hon."

Chapter Five

As soon as she got home after work on Monday, Audie punched the number on the business card Suzanne gave her into her cell phone. Holding the phone between her shoulder and ear, Audie carried her clothes to the laundry hamper and returned to her bedroom. Four rings later, she heard, "Acker Agency."

"Michelle Acker, please."

"You got her."

"Ms. Acker, my name is Audra Wade. I'm Suzanne Travers' business partner."

"How are you, Ms. Wade? It's been a while, but I remember you. What can I do for you?"

"I need to locate someone…as quickly as possible."

"No problem. What's the name and tell me anything you know about the individual."

"Amanda Lange. L-A-N-G-E. Other than that, all I know is she's a blonde, approximately in her late twenties or early thirties. I know it's not much to go on, but I have a photograph of her that was taken a few years ago, if that will help."

"Can you take a picture with your phone and text it to me? That might be easier and quicker."

"Excellent. I'll get it to you this evening. Thanks, and please send the bill to me directly. It's not company related."

"How deep a search are you looking for?"

"If you locate her, I want to speak to her myself involving a personal matter," Audie said, biting back her simmering anger.

****

The next morning, Audie was going over a stack of contracts Suzanne had negotiated during a trip two weeks earlier. Copies would need to be sent to their clients along with a less legal explanation for a few of the more intricate clauses. Any money their company realized from their representation would come from future earnings. Audie was halfway through the stack when Suzanne walked through the open door of Audie's office, shuffling through some mail.

She dropped a small pile of envelopes in front of Audie, then rested her hip on the side of Audie's desk as she used Audie's letter opener on one of the envelopes.

"How's it going?" Suzanne asked absently as she perused the contents.

"I should have them done tomorrow afternoon, I think. Then I'll dictate a more generic version for Linda to enclose with the formal paperwork," Audie said as she leaned back in her chair and ran her hands through her short hair.

"What kind of deadline did you put on them?"

"Three weeks from the date on each contract. I staggered them a little so we wouldn't get all of them back at once. Why?"

Suzanne shrugged slightly. "Just wondering. Anyone you think might give us a problem?"

Audie glanced through the return addresses of her mail before taking the letter opener from Suzanne and slitting each one open. "I'm a little concerned about the girl from middle Tennessee. The impression that I got from our discussion with her and her family was that they would like to see her hold out for more money, initially."

"I sort of got the impression her brother or cousin or whoever the hell he was didn't trust us," Suzanne said and shook her head.

"Everyone else seemed to be pretty amenable to what you negotiated. If we lose one it wouldn't be a tragedy," Audie said absently as she looked at an envelope and flipped it over. It was hand addressed to her in delicate calligraphy and looked like some type of invitation.

"I'd hate to lose that one though," Suzanne said as Audie slid the contents from the envelope. "I think she needs our help, probably more than the others."

Audie unfolded a piece of paper from the envelope and stared at it, her eyes widening slightly. The paper said simply: *Stay away from her!* "Shit," she said mostly to herself.

"What?" Suzanne asked as she continued to peruse her own mail.

Audie quickly refolded the paper and slid it back into the envelope. "Nothing. Just another fundraiser."

"You coming over Friday night?"

"I suppose I'll have to, or I'll never hear the end of it from Gia."

"She just wants you to be your old self again, Audie. You know, annoying but happy." Suzanne grinned.

"Well, that's not very likely, is it?" Audie said with a hint of irritation in her voice. "Just tell her to back off, okay?"

"Come to her little gathering, and you can tell her yourself. I'm not getting in the middle of this."

"Coward."

"Damn straight, girlfriend. I can afford to piss you off. I'm not sleeping with you."

Audie laughed then said, "You are truly pussy whipped, Suzanne. Never thought I'd live to see that."

"Oh, and you think you weren't?"

"I guess that's a small price to pay for what you think is love," Audie said quietly.

"Frankly, I think you've been celibate too damn long. It's making you grumpier than normal. And speaking of grumpy, I'm going to go home early and see if I can talk Gia into making me less grumpy before dinner. I do some of my best work when I'm hungry," Suzanne said, waggling her eyebrows. "See you tomorrow."

Audie laughed at Suzanne's innuendo. "Tell Linda to go home, too. I have a few things left to do here and can answer the phone if it rings."

With a wave of her hand, Suzanne left Audie's office. A few minutes later, Audie heard voices in the reception area, followed by footsteps and the click of the lock on the front doors to their offices. Suddenly everything was eerily silent. Audie retrieved the calligraphied envelope and removed the paper again.

Stay away from her!

Rubbing her temples with her fingertips, Audie tried desperately to think of who she might need to stay away from, but no one came to mind. It occurred to her that it could be from a disgruntled relative of one of their clients, but the postmark was local and they weren't actively trying to recruit any female Longhorn athletes. She thought the brief note must have been meant for someone else, but it was clearly addressed to her office and whoever sent it used her proper name, so obviously it was intended for her.

Chapter Six

Just to prove Gia wrong, Audie decided to attend their little Friday night soiree, but when she pulled into the driveway, a vision of Carlie seated beside her and smiling stopped her from getting out of the car. While Audie could dismiss her own discretion by telling herself it was grief fueled, she could never forget the stab in her heart created by Carlie's affair.

Audie's mind was still embroiled with her personal turmoil, and she was frowning when Suzanne opened the door.

"Well, we're looking all kinds of cheerful tonight," Suzanne said as she took Audie's platter.

"I developed a headache on my way over," Audie said and followed Suzanne into the house.

"Well, grab a beer while I add this to the collection," Suzanne said on her way to the kitchen.

As Audie walked into the game room, she was greeted by several friends she and Carlie shared, but none she knew well. It was well over a fucking year ago, and they were still expressing their condolences. She grabbed a beer from the bar and thought maybe this hadn't been such a good idea after all.

There were a few new faces that caught her attention as she surveyed the room. She wondered what her friends' reactions would be if she just found someone and put the moves on them. The thought made her smile. Maybe Suzanne was right. Surely, they didn't expect her to mourn for the rest of her life and lock herself away in a state of celibacy. Finally deciding that enough was enough, Audie strolled across the room toward a new face.

"Shoot a game?" she asked, indicating the vacant pool table.

"Sure," the woman said and smiled. She was slender and reasonably attractive with blonde hair feathered around her face, resembling a Farrah Faucet throwback.

Audie placed her hand on the small of the woman's back and escorted her toward Suzanne's pool table. "Audie Wade," she said.

"Jenny McClain."

"I haven't seen you at any of these gatherings before."

"I came with Lynda Harrelson. We work together."

Audie estimated Jenny at approximately forty, close enough to her own age.

"Well, welcome to the group. I'll rack." Audie smiled.

Jennie played a hell of a good game, even though there wasn't much conversation.

"I'll play the winner," a familiar voice said.

"Your funeral," Audie said as she looked up into Reagan's blue-gray eyes before sinking the eight ball.

"I've got twenty that says I can take you," Reagan said and then reached into the back pocket of her form-fitting jeans.

"Rack 'em." Audie took a moment to scan the exposed expanse of skin showing along Reagan's midriff.

"I should warn you," Reagan said, flashing a brilliant smile at Audie. "I hate to lose."

"Yeah, well, I hate broccoli, but that doesn't mean I don't get stuck choking it down from time to time."

At some point during their pre-game sparring, Jenny drifted away. Reagan lifted the rack from the balls and took a drink of her beer as she stepped back for Audie to break. A solid ball fell into the side pocket, and Audie walked confidently around the table looking for her best shot. Since Reagan threw down a challenge, Audie was more than willing to let her competitiveness blossom.

Four balls later, Audie missed a difficult bank shot into a side pocket and had to turn the table over to Reagan. Audie picked up her beer and leaned against the wall as Reagan surveyed her options. Audie smiled to herself as Reagan leaned over the table to line up her first shot. The view from where Audie was standing wasn't half bad, and she considered asking for a handicap due to the distraction caused by Reagan's pleasantly rounded ass.

Reagan studied each shot carefully. She never spoke and seemed to be oblivious to anyone watching her. She carried herself with a confidence that Audie liked and, from the cut of the tank top she was wearing, wasn't self-conscious about her body in the least. Audie couldn't help but catch an occasional glimpse of the barbed wire tattoo that encircled Reagan's bicep when she stretched her arm out to line up a shot. It was similar to one she'd seen somewhere before, but she couldn't place where.

It wasn't until Reagan was down to her last two balls that Audie's own competitive nature began to really kick in. From the looks of it, she might get one more chance at the table. She'd need to make it good if she expected to win. On her next shot, Reagan's ball rattled in a corner pocket but failed to drop.

"I was robbed, but you better not miss any of your balls or your ass and your money will be mine," Reagan said as she stepped away from the table.

"I'll do my best to make sure that doesn't happen, although it doesn't sound all that terrible a fate," Audie said with a cocky grin and a wink before she leaned her tall frame over the table to line up her shot.

Audie sank her remaining balls but was left with a difficult bank shot the length of the table for the eight ball. As she squatted down, she estimated the angle to the corner pocket before tapping it with her cue and leaning over the cue ball. The second her stick hit the cue ball, Audie knew she'd struck it perfectly and watched the eight-ball drop into the designated pocket.

Reagan walked over and extended her hand.

As Audie took it, she smiled broadly.

"Keep your money," she said.

"I always pay my debts. And besides, I sold a piece today," Reagan said and smiled.

"It really wasn't a fair match, you know. I've probably been shooting pool ten years longer than you have, but you put up a helluva fight."

"I never make excuses for losing. You were just luckier than me...this time."

Much of the remainder of the evening was spent eating and playing poker, a game that Audie also enjoyed. She won a few hands but eventually bowed out, leaving the others to duke it out for the penny ante pot. She had consumed at least three beers and decided that some fresh air would help clear her head before driving home.

Gia and Suzanne had a beautiful back garden, and even though it was slightly chilly, there was no wind, which made it tolerable. She and Carlie had been in their garden many times. They attended a civil union ceremony for two of their friends five or six years earlier and too many summer cookouts to count.

She took a deep, relaxing breath and made her way toward a small gazebo near a koi pond that was filled by a gentle waterfall of recycled water. There was an arched bridge which spanned the pond and ended near the gazebo. It was one of Carlie's favorite places at Suzanne's home. She found the sound of the falling water peaceful and was always amused by the antics of the koi as they waited to be fed.

Maybe Suzanne and Gia were right. Maybe she needed to reconnect with the old friends she and Carlie had. To them, Carlie would always be the cheerful, faithful, caring woman they had always known. They didn't need to know about her indiscretion.

As Audie leaned her hands on the bridge railing and watched the koi swimming lazily within the confines of their man-made pool, she felt a sense of peace sweep through her body. It'd been a long time since she'd thought about Carlie and not become furious.

She tried to trace the whereabouts of Amanda Lange on her own but with little success. Hopefully, Michelle Acker would have more luck. Even if she found her, Audie didn't know what she would say when she confronted the "other" woman. As far as she knew, Carlie had no plans to leave her, and after Carlie died, all the self-doubt and guilt seemed pointless. When she thought about Carlie's betrayal, Audie realized it was mostly her pride that took a serious hit. But the idea of Carlie in another woman's arms, enjoying her body, drove Audie crazy.

Audie pushed away from the bridge railing to return to the house. She was startled to find Reagan standing at the foot of the bridge watching her.

"I didn't mean to scare you," Reagan said.

"You didn't. I was just absorbed in thought and didn't hear

anyone come out of the house," Audie said and smiled.

"May I join you? Suddenly it was beginning to feel a little close inside."

"Of course. My time on the bridge meter has expired anyway," Audie said as she started down the bridge.

"Please don't leave because of me. I'd enjoy a little one-on-one conversation. My ears tend to get overwhelmed by two or three people all talking at once, and it seems much more peaceful out here."

Audie shrugged as Reagan came up the gentle rise of the bridge and stood next to her, looking down at the koi.

"They're beautiful...so serene," Reagan said quietly.

"Not a care in the world except where their next handout is coming from," Audie said wistfully.

"You didn't look very happy when I first noticed you out here. Is there anything I can do?"

"I was just remembering something that isn't one of my better memories. It happens occasionally," Audie said as she leaned forward and rested her forearms on the bridge railing.

"Thinking about jumping in and ending it all?" Reagan asked with a soft laugh.

"Only if I wanted to drown my ankles." Audie laughed and then looked over her shoulder at Reagan and smiled. "Thanks."

"For what?"

"For making me forget what I was thinking about."

Audie was surprised when Reagan gently ran her hand across her back and patted her shoulder lightly. "You'll get my bill in a few days."

"Maybe I could repay you by taking you to dinner sometime."

"Ah, the old barter system. I'll consider it. Are we talking burgers and fries or surf and turf?"

"Since I am feeling so much better, I suppose there would at least be steak involved. You do like steak, don't you?"

"Born and raised in Texas. What do you think?"

"Hmm. Sounds like you might enjoy enchiladas with Spanish rice and a Corona with lime, too. No, wait, that would be me. I was born and raised in New Mexico."

"Ah, the Land of Enchantment," Reagan said and sighed. "Why did you leave?"

"It isn't as enchanting as you might think, and I was offered a scholarship that I couldn't refuse."

"Sounds like an interesting story."

Standing upright again, Audie said, "Maybe for another time. Would you like to sit in the gazebo for a while?"

"Sure," Reagan said and smiled.

As Audie looked at Reagan, she could feel the beginning of a knot forming in the pit of her stomach. Choosing to ignore the feeling, she walked to the gazebo and sat down. She leaned back against the railing, stretched her long legs out, and took another deep breath. Reagan took a small, self-guided tour of the gazebo and looked over the railing at the gardens Gia had planted around it. Finally, she ended her tour in front of Audie.

When Audie met her gaze, Reagan asked softly, "What are you thinking about right now?"

"That it's peaceful here and I like that." Audie sighed as Reagan's eyes trapped hers, and she felt the unfamiliar sensation of the knot in her stomach growing and beginning to spread through her body.

Reagan sat next to Audie, letting her hand rest easily on Audie's thigh. Breath caught in Audie's throat at the touch, and she hoped the surprise didn't show on her face.

"Do you have another exhibit planned?" Audie asked as a way to fill the dangerous silence that was gathering around them.

Suddenly, and to Audie's relief, Reagan became more animated. "As a matter of fact, there is a gallery in Santa Fe that has expressed an interest in showing a few of my paintings and two or three metal sculptures as long as they have a Southwestern theme."

"That would be a good venue, wouldn't it?"

"If it were successful it could lead to other offers farther west," Reagan explained excitedly.

She left her hand on Audie's thigh and ran the nail of her index finger along the inseam of Audie's jeans. With each movement, Audie felt her body react. Carlie would do the same thing because she knew the feel of her fingernail slowly dropping over each stitch in Audie's jeans would eventually drive Audie crazy. Now she was just trying to drive the feeling out of her mind, without much success.

"There's a wonderful gallery near the Governor's Palace in the Plaza at Santa Fe. I was there a few years ago and found the work being produced by local artists very stimulating," Reagan continued, her finger stroking relentlessly along Audie's inseam.

"Would you please not do that," Audie managed to choke out.

"Not do what?" Reagan asked, a sly smile playing along her lips.

"You know fucking well what," Audie said as she stopped Reagan's hand from moving and frowned.

"Does it offend you?"

"No, but I...I'm not interested in..."

Reagan turned her body toward Audie. Her hand continued to travel up Audie's leg to her crotch. "Your body seems to disagree, and I think you're more than interested," she breathed as her lips met Audie's briefly. She smiled when Audie gasped. Reagan pressed her hand more demandingly between Audie's thighs.

Audie wanted to accept Reagan's blatant sexual advance, but something was stopping her. A thousand thoughts fought with one another in her mind. Audie was flattered to have the attention of such an attractive young woman. Opening her eyes, she looked calmly at Reagan, running her fingers into the silken curls of Reagan's light hair.

Now that she was so aroused, she knew she wouldn't be able to resist and needed to do what she had always done and take control of what was happening. Audie drew Reagan closer to her and covered her mouth with her own, her tongue expertly probing inside. Reagan wrapped her arms tightly around Audie's neck and deepened the kiss.

Reagan breathed heavily and pulled her mouth away and gazed deeply into Audie's eyes. She trailed her mouth and tongue along Audie's neck.

"Reagan...," Audie said.

Before Audie could get more out, Reagan dropped her hand to Audie's crotch again, and Audie arched against her touch.

"Damn," Reagan breathed hotly against Audie's ear. "You're so hot, baby."

"Slow down, kid," Audie forced herself to say hoarsely as her fingers encircled Reagan's wrist to pull her hand away.

"Why?" Reagan asked, her eyes slightly unfocused and hazy. "I like you."

Audie cleared her throat. "I like you, too, but I'm not ready for…this. I'm sorry, kid, but it's too soon for me."

Audie saw a flicker of hurt harden Reagan's eyes as she stood. "I'm a patient woman, so perhaps we'll meet again in the future when you feel more ready," Reagan said before walking resolutely over the bridge, back toward the house.

Audie buried her fingers in her hair as she leaned forward and held her head in her hands. "Damn," she muttered before forcing herself to stand on still shaky legs and re-enter the house, going immediately to the bathroom to splash cold water on her face.

She looked at herself in the mirror and realized for the first time in her life she had not been the aggressor. When she came out of the bathroom, she found Reagan in the kitchen laughing and chatting with Gia, looking as if nothing unusual had happened. There was no reaction from her as Audie caught her eye for a moment. After saying her goodbyes to Suzanne and a few others, Audie took her jacket from the coat rack and left.

It was past midnight when Audie finally arrived home. Whatever alcohol she'd consumed at Suzanne's had long since left her body, but her head pounded. She couldn't wait to strip out of her clothes and stand under the spray in her shower. She needed to wash away the whole evening—the feel of Reagan's searching hands and mouth, the scent of her own arousal, the pungent smell of the unfulfilled promise of sex. By the time she ran most of the hot water out of her system, she was still exhausted and slid gratefully between the cool sheets naked, drifting off to sleep almost immediately. Thankfully, she still had the remainder of the weekend to rest.

* * * *

By late Saturday morning, Audie was tempted to call Reagan but couldn't bring herself to pick up the phone. She wasn't sure she liked the way Reagan made her feel. She hadn't gotten drunk last night, but her head felt like she was fighting a hangover. She pulled on lightweight sweatpants and a sleeveless tank top, slipped her house keys into her pocket, and left her house; she needed to make her body feel something.

She called Buck to accompany her and started off at a leisurely pace as she followed the jogging path she often took, which would take her nearly two miles roundtrip. After only half a mile, she knew she'd put off strenuous exercise for too long.

When Carlie was healthy, she often accompanied Audie on jogs. They would talk about anything that popped into their heads. The sight of Carlie's body glistening with sweat, her chest rising and falling as she caught her breath, never failed to excite Audie.

But Carlie was gone. No amount of wishing could bring her back to fill the terrible aching loneliness or emotional void her death left behind.

Audie's legs were on fire by the time she reached the final curve that led back home, and she resolved to begin running again at least three times a week. Buck would enjoy it, and despite the aching muscles, her body did feel better. She stopped in the middle of her driveway and bent over to catch her breath.

She looked around and realized she should do something about Carlie's gardens. Audie always thought they were beautiful, but she had little or no interest in maintaining them herself. Maybe she could find some minimal care plants to fill them.

She fumbled to extract the door key from the damp pocket of her sweatpants as she walked up the front steps. A quick shower later, she was dressed casually and on her way to Suzanne's.

She smiled when Suzanne opened the door, dressed in basic mid-80's grunge fashion, complete with ancient threadbare jeans and a navy bandana tied around her head.

"Didn't you have those jeans when I first met you?" Audie asked as her eyes surveyed Suzanne's still lean body.

"That why you're here? To critique my wardrobe?" Suzanne answered with a laugh.

"No, I just needed to talk about something, if you have

the time."

Suzanne opened the door and motioned Audie inside. "I think I can spare a few minutes for a friend."

As soon as Audie entered the marbled foyer, Gia came out of the kitchen, wiping her hands on a small towel. She smiled when she saw Audie and hugged her, kissing both cheeks. "I have your platter from last night in the kitchen."

"Thanks, Gia. I'll grab it on my way out. I need to borrow Suzanne for a few minutes."

"Is something wrong?"

"No, no. I just need her advice about something."

"Go out to the garden, Suzanna. Can I bring you something to drink, Audra?"

"No, I'm good."

Suzanne led Audie quietly onto the back deck. "I was just working on the pump for Gia's waterfall. Do you mind if I work on it while we talk? I don't want to have to move those damn fish...again."

Audie laughed then said, "Go ahead. I'm the one who wants to talk. You can just listen."

"Well, pull up a rock and hand me the tool I need when I ask for it," Suzanne said as she picked up a screwdriver and squatted next to the hidden water pump.

Taking a deep breath, Audie waited a minute before finally talking. "Something happened at the party last night. Reagan and I were in the gazebo, just talking, when out of nowhere we sort of had...a...a moment."

"What kind of moment?" Suzanne asked, raising an eyebrow.

"Kissing and touching mostly, but it could have easily turned into something more serious. I stopped her, even though I didn't really want to. I couldn't let anything happen, at least not in your backyard. Now I don't know what to say to her. I...think I hurt her feelings, even though I didn't mean to."

"You can't be serious, Audie," Suzanne hissed. "She's a fuckin' baby!"

"Don't you think I know that?" Audie said irritably. "But you thought she was all right when you and Gia introduced us."

"That was as a dinner companion, for Christ's sake, not a

potential lover."

"I've never apologized to a woman before," Audie admitted. "Truthfully, the only woman I've ever been serious about was Carlie. After we met, I knew there was never going to be anyone else for me."

"I know you dated quite a few hot ladies before you met Carlie. Are you telling me you didn't bed any of them?"

Audie shrugged. "Of course I did, but it was never serious. I've never claimed to be a freakin' saint."

"So, that's how you got that lady killer reputation?" Suzanne cocked her head and laughed.

"I guess, but I wasn't the stud they made me out to be. Hell, the first time Carlie kissed me, I thought I'd faint," Audie said and laughed.

"How did you feel when you kissed Reagan?"

"First of all, *she* kissed me," Audie said defensively. "And I was dumb-founded."

"But you didn't discourage her, did you?" Suzanne grinned. "Maybe she's just a kid looking for a woman with...experience. You know, someone without training wheels."

"Could be, but I'm not sure I'm interested in getting involved with anyone yet. It still feels too soon for me. If she was just feeling me out for a quick hook-up, then I probably wouldn't be interested anyway."

"Maybe not, but even to me, you're not bad looking. You're charming, polite, and considerate. A regular Girl Scout."

"You do know you just described my dog, right?" Audie cringed.

Suzanne laughed. "Except he sheds more. If I were you, I'd invite her to dinner or something simple and see how it goes. You never know, she might turn out to be just what you need."

"I'll think about it, but you're probably right. She's too damn young for me." Even as she said the words, Audie wasn't sure she believed them.

Chapter Seven

The phone on Audie's desk buzzed. She punched the blinking line and said crisply, "Travers and Wade."

"Audie Wade, please," an uncertain sounding woman's voice said.

"This is Audra Wade. How may I help you?"

"Great! How are you? Haven't seen you in a while," the woman said. "Are you ignoring me? It's been two weeks."

"I'm sorry. Who is this?" Audie asked suspiciously.

"Reagan. Reagan Malloy. Sounds like I didn't make as much of an impression on you as I'd hoped," she said and chuckled humorously.

"Sorry. I didn't recognize your voice. What can I do for you, Reagan?" Audie asked with a smile as she leaned back into her leather desk chair. Although she was planning to contact Reagan eventually, she was surprised the young artist had taken the initiative to reach out first. Audie remembered the feel of Reagan's lips against hers, soft yet hot and demanding. And she also remembered how unsettled she felt afterward.

"I've been thinking about having a contract drawn up to send to gallery owners to let them know my terms for a show," Reagan said.

"I'm assuming you have an agent or artist representative. Wouldn't they do that for you? I'm not trying to turn away business, but I'm also fairly sure your agent would be much more familiar with the fine art market and be able to provide more specialized service than we could."

"Perhaps I can give you a copy of my last gallery showing contract and have you look over it so I know everything was adequately covered. If you have time, of course."

"I'd be glad to look over it and give you my opinion. Just drop it off at my office and—"

"Or you could come to my place for dinner next weekend.

I'm planning to grill on Saturday, and you could read over the contract then. Then we could discuss it at our leisure," Reagan said softly.

"Well, I'm going out of town tomorrow but should be back in two or three days and don't have anything scheduled on my calendar for next weekend, if that would be agreeable with you."

"Sounds great," Reagan said and gave Audie her address.

"Then I'll look forward to it, Reagan," Audie said and smiled. "What time should I be there?"

"Drop over a little early, around four," Reagan said quickly. "Then I can show you what goes into my work, if you're interested."

"That works for me. Goodbye, Reagan."

"Bye," Reagan said just as Audie disconnected.

Audie shook her head and took a deep breath. She surprised herself by accepting Reagan's invitation to her home but immediately had second thoughts.

She picked up a small stack of contracts, carried them to Suzanne's office, and tapped on the door before entering. Suzanne glanced up at her, and Audie dropped them on Suzanne's desk.

"Reagan Malloy called me today. She wants me to look over her gallery contract for her," Audie said bluntly.

"Doesn't she have an artist's representative?"

"It sounds like she wants a second opinion. She invited me to her house after our next trip to discuss it. I accepted and thought you should know," Audie said, taking a seat across from Suzanne's desk.

Suzanne leaned back. "I'm not your mother, Audie. You don't need my permission to have a date with anyone."

"It's not a date," Audie insisted. "It's a business meeting."

"Call it whatever you want, sweetie, but at least be honest about it."

"The woman is only interested in my legal advice," Audie huffed.

****

The following Saturday, Audie arrived at Reagan's. She

was dressed in a pair of comfortable, faded jeans, a gray, long-sleeve Henley pull-over, and well-worn rough-out desert boots. The small house was a couple of blocks off Loop One on a street lined with older, but well-kept homes. Mature sycamores dotted the sidewalks on either side of the street, and a well-trimmed hedge outlined the sidewalk to the front steps and led to four steps up to the generous front porch. It was nice to see it in the daylight.

Audie was surprised when a young man opened the door. "Is Reagan Malloy here?"

"She's in her studio out back," the man said and took a generous bite from the sandwich in his hand. "I'm her brother, Ian. She said she was expecting company, so don't bother to knock. She probably wouldn't hear it anyway. Just go on in," he added around a mouthful of his sandwich.

"Thanks," Audie said as she stepped from the porch.

She turned the corner of the house and followed a brick walkway toward the back. The studio was actually a converted two-car garage. It was covered with thick English ivy over rustic looking siding. The original garage door was replaced by French doors with stained glass panels on either side of the doors. Newly planted gardens were on either side of the walkway and just beginning to take hold in the early spring weather.

Even through the doors, Audie could hear loud music and a heavy crackling sound. She opened the door slowly and gazed into the studio. Sparks flew in front of Reagan, who stood at the far end of a large workbench that covered most of the room's interior space. Bins full of various materials and shelves lined three walls.

Audie watched as Reagan worked, not wanting to startle her. As she waited, she looked around the studio at pieces in various stages of completion. Welding seemed to be an unlikely genre for a woman like Reagan. The crackling stopped abruptly, followed by the hissing sound of the cooling welding torch alone. Audie glanced toward Reagan, who had turned the torch off and flipped her welding mask up on her head.

"See anything you like?" Reagan asked.

"Yeah, I saw the piece you sold Suzanne last week," Audie

said, blushing slightly. "It made me curious about how you create these sculptures."

"Did you like it?" Reagan asked as she pulled her leather gloves off and tossed them on the workbench.

"It was very…interesting." Audie nodded, the image of the sculpture of two figures intimately entwined popping up in her mind.

"It should look nice on their patio once Suzanne has the lights installed. It's not one of my personal favorites, but everyone has their own tastes." Reagan laughed quietly.

"Working on a new one?"

"No, I'm taking this one apart. It wasn't working for me. It goes that way sometimes. You try something new and later decide you don't like it as much as you thought you might. But, like many things in life, you never know what you'll like until you give it a try," Reagan said with a smile, then opened a small refrigerator beneath the workbench. "Beer?"

"No, thanks."

"When did you get back?"

"Late last night," Audie said and smiled.

"Tired?"

"Not very. I slept in later than usual this morning."

Reagan set her drink down and walked toward Audie. Audie felt Reagan's blue-gray eyes bore into hers. "Are you *hungry*, Audie?" Reagan asked with a slow smile as Audie watched the tip of Reagan's tongue slide over her lips while her fingers ran down the center of Audie's chest. "Or, if you're curious, I can show you how I create my sculptures."

"Show me. I had a late lunch." Audie swallowed with a grin, mildly aroused by the look in Reagan's eyes and the touch of heat from her fingers.

For the next half hour, Audie watched Reagan form pieces of metal into rough art. Finally, Reagan stopped and turned her torch off, flipping her face shield up.

"Where'd you learn to weld?" Audie asked.

"High school automotive class. Repairing radiators isn't the only thing they teach. Welding was part of the curriculum. I had the neatest welds in my class," Reagan said proudly. "Want me to show you how?"

"Sure, but I'm afraid I'm probably more the radiator repair

type." Audie chuckled. "Not very artistic."

"Put on my apron, gloves, and mask. Just do what I tell you to do, and you'll be fine," Reagan instructed. She brushed a clear substance on two pieces of metal and handed one to Audie, telling her where to place it. She sparked a torch starter and stepped away. Audie brought the flame to the metal and attached the pieces as Reagan reached around her to steady her forearm.

"Don't be afraid," Reagan said. She brushed more pieces and let Audie weld them together, eventually creating a simple flower.

Audie turned the torch off and flipped the welding mask up to examine what she'd made. She smiled broadly. "I've never created anything before. Pretty amateurish though. Thank you," she said.

"It'll be beautiful once it's ground smooth and painted," Reagan said, running her hand softly down Audie's back.

"Hot work," Audie said and unfastened the heavy leather apron protecting her chest.

"You should try it without air conditioning." Reagan laughed.

"Pass." Audie grinned.

"Pussy," Reagan teased. "You seem a little pre-occupied today. Rough trip?"

"Not too bad. I just have a lot on my mind, I guess. Sorry."

"Like what?"

"I'm mostly trying to think of a way to apologize for what happened at Suzanne's. I'm sorry if I did or said anything to upset you because that wasn't my intention."

"You have nothing to apologize for. I wasn't upset and, really," Reagan said quietly and shrugged, "Nothing happened."

"I've never done anything like that before, except with my wife."

"Did you regret it?"

Audie placed the apron, gloves, and mask on the workbench. "My only regret was that it reminded me of her."

"Did she hurt you?"

"Yes," Audie struggled to admit. "I found out after she died that she cheated on me." Tears pooled in Audie's eyes, but she fought to blink them away. "And I, like an idiot, never suspected a thing."

"I think you need to be here, Audie," Reagan said, standing in front of her and kissing her lightly. "Don't go." Reagan breathed softly when the kiss ended. "I haven't been able to get you out of my mind, and you should know that I don't take rejection well." Reagan leaned in for another kiss.

Audie stopped her. "I think we should slow down a little. I'm only here to discuss your current contract with you. It's probably old-fashioned, but I'd like to get to know you better before...we go any further," Audie managed, her breath mingling with Reagan's as she looked into her eyes. "Maybe, for now, I should just help you prepare dinner," she said and smiled.

Reagan took Audie's hand and led her out of the workshop. Audie followed her up the back steps into a large kitchen. While Audie looked around, Reagan began pulling various items out of the refrigerator and setting them on the kitchen island.

Reagan turned to look at Audie. "Can you be trusted to prepare a salad?"

"I think I can manage that. It's easier than welding. What do you prefer in yours?" Audie asked, pulling a knife from a butcher block holder.

"Surprise me." Reagan smiled then opened two packages of quartered chicken and cut a dozen fresh lemons in half. "Make three salads. A friend of mine might be stopping by later." She pressed each half of the lemons into a juicer and got as much juice as possible from each. She dumped the juice into a saucepan, seeds and all, and added a stick and a half of butter. After the butter was melted, she stirred the butter and lemon juice together and set it off the stove. She walked up behind Audie and placed her hands on Audie's hips, peering over her shoulder and squeezing her waist lightly. "Looks good," Reagan said, tickling the edge of Audie's ear with the tip of her tongue.

"I have a knife in my hand, you know," Audie said as she rubbed her ear against her shoulder.

"Yeah, I noticed that," Reagan hummed. "Am I distracting you?"

Audie turned to face Reagan, holding her hands up to stop the tomato juice on her hands from dripping on the floor. "I thought we agreed to take things slowly."

"Yeah, well, that was what *you* wanted, but it doesn't mean *I'll* stop touching you when the mood strikes me. Nothing has to happen beyond that, but I wouldn't object if you felt the need to touch me occasionally. What can I say, I'm an affectionate person. Can't help it," she said and grinned. "So, live with it."

Before Reagan could turn away, Audie pulled her into her arms and kissed her deeply, possessively. Reagan's fingers tangled in Audie's hair as she eagerly returned the kiss, pressing her body against Audie and slipping her tongue between Audie's lips. Audie sucked Reagan's tongue farther into her mouth, stroking it with her own.

When Audie brought the kiss to an end, Reagan pressed her forehead against Audie's chest, took a deep breath, and breathed out, "Damn, baby."

Audie smiled and said, "Now go fix your chicken. The salads will be finished in a minute, and I'm suddenly…ravenous."

****

An hour into their prep work, Audie heard the distinct rumble of a motorcycle pull into the driveway and assumed it was Reagan's friend. A few minutes later, Audie watched the driver of the motorcycle stroll around the side of the house. She was dressed in black jeans and wore a black Harley-Davidson T-shirt under her black leather jacket. Completing her ensemble were heavy-looking black boots.

She stopped next to a cooler, leaned down, and grabbed a Corona, which she popped open with an opener attached to the wall of Reagan's workshop. She inserted a wedge of lime in to the bottle and sucked down a long drink before turning her attention to Reagan and Audie who were relaxing side-by-side on chaise lounges on Reagan's small patio.

Reagan stood and greeted her guest with a warm hug. "I figured you'd show up, Tracey, so grab a table. Dinner will be ready in a few minutes."

"I didn't tell you I was coming over tonight for sure," Tracey said. Glancing at Audie and squinting slightly, she added, "If I'd known you had company, I'd have stayed home."

"Tracey, this is Audie Wade. I invited her over to discuss a business matter," Reagan said.

"She another artist?" Tracey asked.

"No," Reagan said and laughed. "She's an attorney. I needed someone to look over the contract I usually sign before an exhibit, to make sure I'm not getting screwed." Turning to Audie, Reagan said, "This is my best friend, Tracey Chaisson. It's Saturday night, and she usually drops by to see what I'm doing. You might remember her as the woman who elbowed you in our pick-up basketball game a few weeks ago."

Audie stood and extended her hand. "My ribs remember her very well," she said with a tight smile.

"Sorry about that," Tracey mumbled as she took Audie's hand. "Got a little carried away." Tracey wandered over to stand next to Reagan while she flipped the chicken on the grill. "Smells great, Reag," she said, resting her arm across Reagan's shoulders, pulling her closer.

Audie watched the affectionate interaction between Reagan and her friend. In fact, to Audie, Tracey seemed a little too affectionate, but who was she to question the way old friends acted toward one another. It hadn't been that long since Reagan had readily welcomed Audie's kiss.

It wasn't long until the chicken was ready. Audie went into the kitchen to get their salads out of the refrigerator. Soon they were digesting flame grilled lemon-butter chicken and loaded garden salads, too busy eating to talk much.

"Best meal I've had all week, Reagan. Thank you," Tracey said, leaning back in her chair and downing the remainder of her beer.

"Glad you enjoyed your meal," Reagan mumbled as she reached over and took Audie's hand and played with her fingers.

Audie noticed the frown on Tracey's face as she glared at them. "What do you do for a living, Tracey?"

"Freelance computer work for small businesses," Tracey said with a smile. "I won't get rich, but I earn enough to keep me happy. Beats working for a big company, and I make my own rules."

Audie smiled as she interlaced her fingers with Reagan's, then brushed her thumb over the back of her hand as their eyes met.

"This kinda reminds me of Emily," Tracey said.

"Why would you say that?" Reagan asked with a frown, releasing Audie's hand.

"She used to enjoy little cookouts like this. Then you two used to cuddle up for a private moment. Remember?" Tracey said as she stretched. "Still can't believe she ended it the way she did."

Reagan stared hard at Tracey. "I don't think she did. I think someone helped her."

"How can you think that? The coroner found pills and alcohol in Em's stomach."

"Then he was wrong. He didn't know her like we did. It took her forever to decide where to eat dinner, so I'll never believe she would have suddenly decided on a whim that life wasn't worth living any longer," Reagan said adamantly. "I'll never believe it."

"Maybe you're right, Reag, but as long as the cops think it was a suicide, they're not gonna re-open Em's case. Better to not make yourself crazy thinking about what could have happened. Listen, sweetie, dinner was great, as usual, but I'm a little tired so I'm gonna go home and crash. Besides, I think your guest is already asleep."

"I'm glad you made it over tonight, Trace."

Audie opened her eyes enough to see the two friends hug one another. She watched Tracey run her hands slowly down Reagan's back and drop a light kiss on her temple. To Audie, their hug appeared to last longer than a normal embrace before Tracey strolled back to her motorcycle.

After hearing the motorcycle's engine rev and fade away, Audie rolled onto her side and reached out for Reagan's hand. "I'm not asleep. Now that your friend is gone, join me?" she asked, encouraging Reagan to join her on the chaise lounge.

Reagan took Audie's hand and lay down next to her. Audie spooned her body against Reagan's back and curled an arm around her waist to draw her body more snugly against hers.

Reagan ran her hand down Audie's arm until she interlaced their fingers again. Having Reagan in her arms created a familiar feeling, but the body against hers felt different. Audie enjoyed that difference. Reagan's body fit against hers in all the right places, and Audie liked the way her body reacted to their closeness. She felt contented for the first time since she'd lost Carlie.

****

A sudden noise on the street woke Reagan. She looked around but didn't see anything except Audie dozing peacefully beneath her. Reagan lowered her lips to softly kiss Audie and was surprised when Audie's fingers tightened slightly on her neck and pulled her closer to kiss her more insistently. Reagan patted Audie's chest when their lips separated. "I thought you wanted to take things slowly until we know one another better," Reagan said when Audie's eyes opened and met hers.

"I think we should, but there's nothing wrong with a few friendly kisses here and there," Audie said and grinned. "I am human, you know. Sorry I crashed."

"Maybe we were both just tired. You from your trip and me from staying up too many nights to work. And just so you know, you make a really good pillow."

"Thanks. Must be getting soft and fluffy. Maybe the wine I used in the salad dressing combined with the beer we had with dinner wore me out."

"Who cares? I could spend the whole night out here as long as I can use you for my personal pillow." Reagan sighed, putting her head down again. "You have the softest boobs, baby."

Audie laughed. "They're not much to brag about, but if you say so, I can live with soft."

"Think I'll get to see them up close and personal some day?" Reagan asked, waggling her eyebrows.

"Don't rush it, sweetie, but it's a possibility. They're not going anywhere, and I take them with me everywhere."

Reagan pressed her mouth against Audie's chest and nipped one of her breasts playfully. "You're mean," she said and pouted.

Audie patted her on the butt. "Come on, kiddo. I'll help you clean up. I need to get home and feed my dog."

"Okay," Reagan groaned as she pushed herself up. "I'll pack up the leftover chicken for your dog. We never did get around to talking about the contract stuff. You might have to come back tomorrow."

"*Or* I could meet you at our office tomorrow afternoon, if you want," Audie suggested as they walked hand-in-hand into Reagan's kitchen.

"*Or* I could meet you at your house." Reagan grinned as she wrapped the chicken in aluminum foil. "Since you've seen mine, I'd like to see yours," she said and winked. "And I'd love to see that eclectic art collection I've heard so much about and really should meet your dog to see if he approves of me invading his space."

"Okay, but bring your running shoes and shorts. Buck and I run two miles three days a week, and tomorrow is our day to run. Think you're up for it?"

"Hell, yeah! You can't scare me off with the threat of a little exercise," Reagan boasted as she followed Audie to her car and leaned against the SUV, her hand drifting down Audie's arm. She hated running but wouldn't tell Audie that right now. It would be her temporary little secret.

****

Reagan pulled into the circular drive of Audie's long ranch-style home on Sunday afternoon. The home overlooked Lake Travis near the Austin city limits. It seemed to stretch forever until it jutted out at a forty-five-degree angle through a large double lot dotted with huge live oak trees. The branches of the trees provided shade over more than half of the structure, and wide gardens ran beneath the large front windows of the comfortable looking house.

Several windows facing the driveway were either pastoral scenes done in stained glass or had large stained glass pieces centered in them. Reagan stepped onto the covered porch and pushed the doorbell, shoving her hands into the back pockets of her jeans while she waited. When the front door opened, she could feel the cool air emanating from inside, which looked equally cool and refreshing.

Audie stood in front of Reagan, smiling down at her and wearing a bright yellow T-shirt over dark green, nylon running shorts. Reagan smiled back as she took in Audie's long, muscled legs appreciatively. Audie's right hand lightly stroked the blonde fur along the back of a large, inquisitive Labrador Retriever that strained to lean closer and sniff the stranger standing at the entrance of his domain.

"This must be Buck," Reagan said. "May I touch him?"

"He'd like that, but afterward he probably won't leave you alone. He's a sucker for affection," Audie answered.

"Like his owner, huh?" Reagan grinned up at Audie and noticed her face flush as she knelt down to take Buck's big head in her hands. She was rewarded by several quick, wet kisses. Reagan stood and ran her hand over her face. "Sweet guy," she said and laughed.

"Yeah, he really knows how to impress the ladies. Please come in. What would you like to do first, discuss your contract or go for a run?"

"I think I'd like to wash my face and then take a tour of this lovely house. It's beautiful," Reagan said, noticing the warmth created by sunlight as it sent a variety of colors through the stained glass into the front room.

Audie motioned to her right. "Of course. There's a guest bath on the left three doors down the hallway. Can I get you a drink?"

"Just water, please," Reagan said, touching Audie's arm briefly before moving down the wide hallway. She stopped occasionally to examine a picture on the wall more closely. Some were originals by artists whose names she didn't recognize, a few were well-framed lithographs of antique maps, others were photographs, mostly black-and-whites, and taken along a waterfront.

While Reagan washed her face, she wondered why Audie seemed somewhat more distant or reticent compared to the evening before. Perhaps she was being cautious about having another woman in the home she'd shared with her late wife. When Reagan returned to the foyer, she found Audie sitting on a red leather couch in the open living room, resting her forearms on her knees, sipping from a bottle of water.

Reagan plopped down next to Audie and took the bottle from her and drank down a big gulp. She rested a hand on Audie's back and rubbed her face with her free hand. "That's better. Now I'm ready to see your home."

Audie stood and took Reagan's hand, escorting her through the dining room and kitchen.

"You have some top-notch appliances. Cook much?" Reagan smiled.

"We used to, but not so much now," Audie said quietly.

"Is something wrong?" Reagan asked with concern.

Audie shook her head. "Just memories. I slept in longer than usual this morning. Still waiting for all my brain cells to wake up, I guess." Audie smiled at Reagan. "You sure there wasn't something in that chicken last night?"

"Positive." Reagan laughed, shoving her playfully. "I've never had to resort to using drugs with any of my female guests. Show me the rest of the house. Then maybe we can go for a run before we discuss business. That should wake you up," Reagan teased.

Audie led Reagan down the hallway. "Not much down here except a bath, which you've already seen, my office, and the master bedroom."

"You can actually tell a lot about someone by seeing their bedroom, you know," Reagan said, squeezing Audie's hand.

"Like what?"

"Like whether you're a secret slob or a neat freak," Reagan said, studying Audie with a grin. "I'm thinkin' you're a neat freak. I lean more toward secret slob personally."

"Guess I'll need to check out your bedroom someday to confirm that," Audie said, wiggling her eyebrows.

"Anytime you want, baby," Reagan crooned.

As they stepped into the master bedroom, the first thing Reagan saw was a large picture hanging over the king-size bed. "Is that one of Shane Carter's paintings?"

"I guess. I saw it the evening of your exhibit and really liked the vibrant colors and how the running paint formed the figure. It's sort of simple but classy looking to me."

"He'll be thrilled I saw it hanging in someone's home. Usually artists don't know what happens to their work after it's sold. Thank you, sweetie."

After a quick glance at Audie's home office and a guest room, Audie snapped her fingers, and Buck came to her. She ruffled his ears and asked, "You ready for a run, buddy?" He jumped up and happily went to the front door, his nails tapping on the entry tiles as he pranced around. "We can stretch out front."

"Well, honestly, I'm not much of a jogging fan. In fact, I've never really been jogging. So, I might need to take a few more rest breaks than you're used to," Reagan confessed.

Audie shrugged. "Then I guess we could make it a brisk walk. Maybe we can discuss the contract at the same time."

"Buck won't mind?"

"As long as one of us throws a stick he can chase, he won't mind," Audie assured her. "Do you need to change into shorts or something? It might be more comfortable."

"No. I'm good," Reagan said, patting her jean-clad thigh. "These are extremely light material."

The two women walked away from Audie's house with Buck trotting slightly ahead of them as he ferreted out new scents along the way.

When they reached a set of steps that led down to a private beach on the shore of the lake, Audie said, "Let's sit on the bench over there. Carlie and I had it placed here several years ago. We can take a break, and you can tell me what you want included in your contract."

"What's included in the contracts you normally write? I'm pretty clueless when it comes to this," Reagan admitted.

"For our clients there's an introductory section that names Suzanne and me as the sole representatives of the client. No one other than one of us can negotiate the terms of the contract. There's another section covering what is expected of our client as well as their monetary compensation. We insist that the team or company also agrees that the contract is binding if our client is injured and unable to perform as anticipated. Included with that is a report of the athlete's physical condition at the time the contract is negotiated to prove she has no hidden injuries. Stuff like that," Audie explained.

"So, I would have to agree that only my agent can negotiate the terms of the contract for me?"

"That's pretty standard, but the artist should be aware of every point covered with a potential gallery that wants to display their work. Every decision should be approved by the artist. I suggest that your representative actively approach galleries and provide them with photographs of your work. You might need some type of protection clause in the event of a cancellation for some capricious reason by the gallery owner."

"Artists usually have to agree to attend a gallery exhibit of their works. Could the contract have a provision for travel, accommodations, and food allowance, within reason, of course, for out-of-town or out-of-state exhibits?"

"I don't think that would be a problem." Audie smiled.

"I should warn you in advance that gallery owners behave on the premise they are doing us a favor by showing our works, which is basically true. They may fight any conditions placed on them, and if they lose, they will make sure every gallery knows the artist is a pain in the ass. It can kill an artist's reputation."

"If they signed a contract, then the artist or their representative can sue them for breach of contract and possibly defamation. The hardest part is getting them to agree the first time. After that they usually fall in line without much of a struggle."

"What if the gallery has its own contract?" Reagan asked.

"Then your agent would negotiate on your behalf to reach common ground about what's in the best interest of the gallery and the artist. It's risky but usually worth it for the protection it provides."

"Truthfully, this might be a hard sell for most artists. None of us are rolling in money since most are at the beginning of their careers and one that their parents warned them probably would never be lucrative." Reagan laughed.

"At least it gives you something to think about when you're more established." Audie stood up and offered her hand to Reagan. "Ready to head back?" she asked, whistling for Buck.

Reagan took Audie's hand as they began making their way up the steps to the top of the hill that would lead them back to Audie's home. Audie released Reagan's hand to pick up a stick for Buck and threw it as far as she could. Buck took off, leaving a puff of dust in his wake. When Audie rejoined Reagan, she draped her arm over her shoulders, and Reagan slid an arm around Audie's waist, hooking her thumb in the elastic waistband of her shorts.

"You do know we live in the bicycle capital of Texas, right?" Reagan asked, looking up at Audie. "Maybe the next time you feel like exercising we can take a nice leisurely bike ride."

"That might be fun. Do you have anything planned for next weekend?" Audie asked.

"Nope," Reagan answered softly. "Why?"

"We…I own a little place on the coast, and I haven't really spent any time there since my wife died. I thought I might drive down next weekend. Buck loves it there. If you're interested, maybe you would consider joining us."

"Probably still too cool to jump in the Gulf water."

"Probably," Audie muttered, looking slightly dejected.

"Is there a fireplace?"

"Yeah."

"Then we can walk on the beach and get a fire going to warm us up. Oh, and hot chocolate with those little marshmallows. Yummy!" Reagan grinned. "Sounds like heaven to me, Audie, as long as you don't mind building a fire."

"Sounds like a definite plan. When do you want us to pick you up?"

"Whenever you're ready. Just give me a call to let me know you're on your way."

Chapter Eight

Early the following Saturday morning, Audie loaded Reagan's two small suitcases in the back of her SUV before settling behind the steering wheel to start their trip.

Reagan opened a drawstring bag on the floorboard. "I made blueberry scones last night, but we might have to stop and get a couple coffees."

"Starbucks?"

"There's a McDonald's right before you get onto the loop. The nearest Starbucks is closer to downtown, and it's a pain to get back to the loop."

"McDonald's is fine," Audie said as she signaled to turn into the drive-thru.

While they waited in line, Reagan took another wrapped package from the bag on the floorboard and maneuvered her body to reach into the back seat. "I made a special scone for Buck. Is it okay if I give it to him?"

"What is it?" Audie asked.

"Bacon, mostly." Reagan smiled.

"I'm sure he'll love you forever then." Audie smiled back as Reagan tore the scone into four pieces and offered one to Buck. He sniffed it briefly before taking the bite into his mouth and swallowing it.

"It would last longer if you took the time to at least pretend to chew it, buddy," Reagan admonished the dog.

Audie glanced in the rearview mirror to see him run his tongue over his jowls. His expressive brown eyes flicked between Reagan and the tempting treat in her hand.

Audie pulled forward and took two large cups of coffee and requested creamer and sugar before handing one to Reagan and setting hers into a holder in the console.

"Want me to add cream and sugar to yours?" Reagan asked.

"Two sugars and two creamers," Audie said. "Thank you."

By the time they pulled onto the loop, Reagan had placed a napkin on Audie's thigh and rested a scone on it. Audie took a bite of her scone and followed it with a swallow of coffee, humming her delight. "Very good," she said around the bite she was chewing.

"My grandmother's recipe. She made the best scones ever," Reagan said, nibbling at her scone and occasionally offering Buck another bite. "Do you have any music with you?"

Audie slid open a ceiling door above the windshield. "Take your pick, but I'm not sure there's anything you might be interested in. It's mostly instrumental stuff we used as background music while we talked. Or I think the car came with a streaming service, if you'd prefer that. Your choice. Sorry."

"No, it's fine," Reagan said as she looked through the CDs. "Which one's your favorite?"

Audie reached up and pulled a CD down. She handed it to Reagan, who looked at the artist and title before sliding it into the CD player. When the music started, Reagan said, "I've heard this before. Galleries sometimes play it as background music, but I never knew the name of it. It's New Age, isn't it?"

Audie glanced at her to reply, but Reagan's eyes were closed, and her head was leaned back. "Do you like it?"

When no reply came, Audie smiled as she hummed to the music.

Two-and-a-half hours later, Audie shook Reagan's shoulder to let her know they'd arrived. Reagan stretched and rubbed her eyes. "I'm sorry, Audie."

"It was either the music or my sparkling personality," Audie said and chuckled. "Unless you slipped something into your scones."

"More likely because I was up half the night baking those scones to impress you," Reagan said. "I'm more than a welder, you know."

"Buck and I were both impressed." Audie smiled.

"Can you do me a favor?"

"Slap you to make sure you're awake?" Audie guessed.

"No, I'm awake. Can you back up and let me see the approach to your retreat? I can already see it's beautiful, but

I'd love to see how it looks as you approach it."

Audie backed up and returned to the main road, then entered her property once again. "Very impressive," Reagan said. "Now I'm ready to see the inside."

"I might have to open the windows to let some fresh air in. I'm sure it's a little stuffy." Audie stepped out and opened the back door to let Buck out. He dashed around the side of the building and returned a few minutes later, walking a little more sprightly.

Audie opened the French doors on the deck and walked through the rooms, opening windows as she went. Reagan wandered in behind Audie, taking in the layout of the bungalow and its accompanying coastal-inspired art. Audie finally walked back through the house and located Reagan examining a painting of breeze-tossed coastal grass embedded along the top of a sand dune, overlooking the greenish-blue water of the Gulf of Mexico.

Audie stepped up behind Reagan and slid her hands around her waist as she rested her chin on the top of Reagan's head.

"Do you like it?"

"It has such a flowing movement," Reagan said, covering Audie's hands with her own. "It feels like I can actually see and feel the grasses moving. It's breathtakingly beautiful."

"It's the last painting I bought for this house. It just seemed to belong here," Audie said, frowning slightly as she remembered purchasing it as a surprise for Carlie on their anniversary. "It was worth every dime I paid for it."

"Does the artist live here?"

"I have no idea. I found it at a small gallery in Port Aransas." Audie shrugged and then took Reagan's hand. "Let's go for a walk on the beach before it gets too late."

Reagan curled her arm around Audie's and squinted up at the azure sky. Buck trotted ahead of them, periodically breaking up a gathering of squawking seagulls. Reagan turned to Audie when they reached the beach.

"I like your retreat," she said.

"Me, too. That's why I couldn't bring myself to sell it after Carlie died. There were so many good memories here," Audie said thickly.

"Maybe you can make other good memories here now."

"It's a possibility," Audie conceded.

They sat in companionable silence for about an hour before Audie said, "We should get back and unload the car. Then we can run to a little market that's not too far away to pick up a few things for the weekend. Or you can stay here with Buck and continue your exploration of *Casa Ventana*."

"What does that mean?" Reagan laughed.

"I don't know. It's something about a house with a view. Carlie made it up."

Reagan stopped to face Audie. "Maybe we shouldn't have come down here. I think your memories of your wife might still be too close to the surface for you."

"I needed to come back. I've never brought anyone but Carlie here, but she did. This is where she cheated on me. She brought another woman to this special place that was only ours," Audie admitted, almost strangling on the words.

Reagan shoved away from Audie glared at her. "Is that why you brought me here, to pay her back? Because you were planning to cheat on her memory here with *me*?" Reagan asked heatedly.

Audie shook her head. "I wouldn't do that," she pleaded. "I don't think that's who I am. I admit I was hurt. But nothing I do can hurt her now."

"I'm sorry, Audie, but I like you and am trying to figure out why you haven't seemed very happy with me," Reagan said as she ran her hand down Audie's back.

"You drive me crazy, kid." Audie pulled Reagan closer into a light hug. "Be patient with me."

Reagan patted Audie on the chest. "Why don't you run to the store while Buck and I unpack before it gets any later."

"What do you want for dinner?" Audie asked.

"Surprise me," Reagan said with a smile. "It's a mild day, so we could grill on the deck and enjoy the fresh air."

"Well, that doesn't narrow down my choices much."

"If it helps, I'm not a picky eater, though I'm not wild about broccoli."

"Is anyone?" Audie laughed.

Reagan took Audie's hand again as they walked to Audie's SUV. She leaned down and dropped a light kiss on Audie's lips, once she was settled in the driver's seat. "Be careful and see if you can find a bottle of wine to go with dinner."

****

Audie glanced at a message on her cell phone before turning left onto the main road that cut through Mustang Island and led to Port Aransas at the northern end of the narrow barrier island. She'd received a message from Michelle Acker about a week earlier but still hadn't formulated a plan to meet the young woman who'd apparently had a lengthy affair with Carlie and now worked at the Beachcomber's Inn just outside the Aransas Pass city limits.

Thinking about Carlie in the arms of another woman brought Audie's rage and sense of betrayal to the surface again. Audie remembered Carlie's unbridled passion when they made love, the look of abandon on her face as she lost herself in Audie's body, and the sound of Carlie's pleasure as Audie drove her closer and closer to orgasm. The visceral memories haunted Audie.

Without realizing where she was, Audie parked her vehicle and closed her eyes in an attempt to shut out the visions in her mind of Carlie in another woman's arms. What would Carlie be feeling, if she knew Audie brought another woman to their retreat? Would Carlie feel as betrayed as Audie did? Was a buried need for some kind of vengeance the reason she'd brought Reagan to the island, even though she denied it?

When Audie finally forced her eyes open again, she found herself staring at the entrance to the Beachcomber's Inn, a neat, two-story building with a wide front porch topped by a balcony across the second story. A banner adorned with seagulls floating above a strip of sea grass bending under a breeze announced, "An Island Culinary Adventure – Welcome."

After sitting in her vehicle and attempting to calm herself, Audie finally opened the door and stepped out, but she felt her strong legs tremble as she took a step forward. She started up the front steps of the restaurant, pushed her sunglasses up to rest on top of her head, and yanked the front door open, preparing herself mentally to face the battle of her life.

A young woman at the front desk smiled winningly when

Audie approached. "Table for one, ma'am, or will others be joining you?" Most of the interior tables were occupied with people who seemed to be enjoying their meals. Audie inhaled the delicious scents wafting from the kitchen.

"It smells great, but I'm not really here to eat," Audie managed to say. "I was hoping to speak to Amanda Lange, if possible."

"Amanda's in the kitchen. She's our chef. Give me a few minutes, and I'll see if she's free enough to come up front. May I tell her who wishes to speak to her?"

Audie cleared her throat and announced clearly, "Audra Wade."

Audie saw what she thought was a flicker of recognition pass over the young woman's face before she left and meandered between tables, stopping periodically to speak to a guest or refill a drink. Audie rested an elbow on the reception desk to gather her thoughts, slapping herself mentally. Just confront her, dammit. Don't embarrass yourself by starting an argument or punching her in the face, no matter how much you want to. This isn't a gym or basketball court, for God's sake.

A few minutes later, the young woman left the kitchen for a moment, then caught the swinging door and leaned back inside. She plastered a smile on her face and made her way back to the reception desk. "Amanda's completing a special entrée at the moment and can't leave it. However, if you'd like to wait at the bar, she should be free to speak to you in ten or fifteen minutes," the woman said. "Please enjoy a drink on the house, for your inconvenience, Ms. Wade," she added.

Audie ordered a double shot of Hennessey over ice, carrying it to a nearby booth. She took a healthy drink to help her relax, wondering if coming to the Beachcomber's Inn had been such a good decision after all. Did she really want to meet her wife's secret lover face-to-face? She considered finishing her drink and leaving, but before she reached a final decision, a slender woman slid into the booth opposite her and removed the hat that covered her long blonde hair.

"What can I do for you, Ms. Wade?" the woman smiled, fluffing her hair slightly.

After almost two years of waiting and wondering, Audie steeled herself and said harshly, "Nothing in particular. I was just curious to meet the woman who had an affair with my wife." The look on Amanda's face was one of shock.

"I assure you, Ms. Wade, I haven't had an affair with your, or anyone else's, wife," Amanda snapped angrily, standing up. "I'm afraid you've wasted your time and mine."

Audie stood up and blocked Amanda's path when she took a step forward. Audie snatched the picture of Carlie with Amanda standing behind her, hugging her affectionately, from her back pocket. Leaning closer, Audie ground out, "*This* is a picture of my wife, Carlie, and unless I'm mistaken, *you* are the woman with her arms wrapped around her."

Amanda gently took the picture and smiled. "It was such a beautiful day," she said softly. "My sister, Christina, was with us and took this picture." She looked up at Audie. "I haven't seen this picture in...a long time," she said and smiled. "How is Carlie?"

"She's dead," Audie rasped bluntly, clinching her hands into fists and struggling to maintain her composure.

"Oh, my God," Amanda said, collapsing back into the booth with tears in her eyes. "When?"

"About eighteen months ago." Audie's face hardened as she glowered at Amanda. "Are you going to continue to lie to me about your affair with Carlie?"

Amanda motioned to the bartender, who nodded. A few moments later, the bartender set a glass in front of her. She took a drink, and with tears in her eyes said, "Carlie was a beautiful, loving woman, but she wasn't my lover. She was my...my mother."

"Your mother? You're lying!" Audie hissed angrily, leaning over Amanda. "We were together twenty-four fucking years, and she didn't have any children. I think I would have noticed a child skipping around our house. She would *never* have kept something like that from me."

"Well, I'm twenty-eight, so do the math," Amanda snapped back. "Perhaps you didn't know her as well as you thought you did." She threw the remainder of her drink down her throat, stood up, and quickly strode away.

****

"This should be a great dinner," Reagan said, bumping playfully against Audie when she returned to the bungalow. "You've been gone nearly three hours."

"It took me a while to decide what to grill," Audie mumbled. "And then to find the right kind of wine to go with it. Sorry."

"Are you okay, Audie?"

"Sure. I'm great. Why wouldn't I be?" Audie answered irritably.

"I've seen you look happier." When Audie pulled a package from a brown paper bag, Reagan's face lit up. "Oh, I love shrimp."

Audie forced a smile in return. "They're supposed to be extra-large but might be mixed. I got them from some guy at the pier who swore they were caught in the Gulf early this morning. It doesn't take long for them to cook, so after I get them cleaned and soaking in a marinade, perhaps you'd like to go for another walk along the beach with me," Audie said, hoping a walk would take her mind off her brief, heated conversation with Amanda Lange.

"I'd love to take another stroll on the beach with you." Reagan threw her arms around Audie and hugged her. "I can tell you about my exciting day with Buck, and you can tell me what's made you a grumpy Gus."

"I already told you nothing is wrong," Audie said and frowned.

"And I know that's not true," Reagan said, taking Audie's face in her hands. "You already know I care about you, so I can handle almost anything, baby, as long as you don't lie to me."

"I won't. I just saw something in town today that upset me. It was nothing important. I promise," Audie said, hugging Reagan and staring out at the dark water and gathering clouds over the Gulf.

Chapter Nine

Following an hour's stroll along the beach, Audie lit torches around the deck to illuminate the grill while Reagan went inside to prepare a rice side dish and a salad. She returned half an hour later to set up folding tables beside their deck chairs. Reagan moved to stand behind Audie and ran her hands slowly up Audie's broad back.

"You're awfully quiet this evening," Reagan said softly.

"Just a little tired," Audie said and shrugged. "Could be from our long walk on the beach and the smell of fresh air blowing in off the Gulf. That always relaxes me."

"I don't know what's in that marinade, but it smells fabulous."

"Open the wine, will you? This should be done in another minute."

They enjoyed glasses of the zesty Sauvignon Blanc Audie brought to accompany the grilled shrimp while they waited for the food to be done. It wasn't long before they were seated and enjoying their meal.

Once finished, Reagan reached for Audie's hand and twined their fingers. "Mind if I join you?"

"Of course not," Audie replied as she scooted over to make room for Reagan.

Reagan took Audie's wine glass and set it on the table before stretching out next to her and rolling over to face her. She buried her face against Audie's neck and began kissing her lightly before raising her head to cover Audie's mouth in a deep, passionate, probing kiss. When she pulled her lips away, Reagan whispered, "Jesus, I've been wanting to do that all day."

Audie slipped her hand beneath Reagan's blouse, and her fingertips brushed lightly across bare breasts.

Whatever might have happened next was interrupted by the sound of a vehicle making its way down the short road to the bungalow. Audie looked up to see a silhouette step out of an older model Ford Bronco.

"Who is it, Audie?" Reagan asked. "Were you expecting company?"

"No, but whoever it is, their timing sucks." Audie exhaled as she stood. "Let Buck out, please," she added in a low voice.

Reagan got up and opened the deck doors, and Buck charged outside to greet the uninvited stranger. The figure dropped to its knees and wrapped its arms around Buck, who began whining, his tail wagging furiously in the sand. "Hey, buddy," a woman's voice laughed. "It's been a long time, huh, pal. I know, I know, I've missed you too, Buckeroo."

Then the figure stood and walked up the steps of the deck and into the flickering light from the torches.

"What the hell are *you* doing here?" Audie snapped, standing to face Amanda Lange.

"I didn't like the way our talk ended this afternoon. Sorry it's a little late, but I had to close the restaurant before I could get away." Still staring at Audie, Amanda stepped forward, extending her hand with a smile toward Reagan. "I'm sorry. I'm Amanda Lange."

Reagan accepted the offered hand briefly. "Reagan Malloy."

"What the fuck do you want?" Audie growled.

"To talk. You said that was what you wanted this afternoon, but now you'll also have to listen...to the truth," Amanda said. "And I'm not leaving until you do. It's what Carlie would want, and you know it."

"Carlie and I didn't keep secrets from each other," Audie spat. "I know you're a liar!"

"Well, it looks like she kept this secret...for almost thirty years," Amanda retorted.

"Would you like a glass of wine?" Reagan asked inanely, out of nowhere.

Audie looked at her like she'd lost her mind and said harshly, "She won't be here long enough for that. This is a personal matter and doesn't involve you, Reagan."

"I think it does, Audie," Reagan said, standing and running her hand down Audie's tense arm. "Because I care about you and something is tearing you up inside. You need for it to heal, sweetie, before you can move forward with your life. Please."

Audie swung around quickly, jabbing her finger in Reagan's face, fighting unsuccessfully to control her fragile emotions. But Reagan didn't flinch. Instead, she stepped closer to Audie and embraced her while angry tears filled Audie's eyes. "She...betrayed...me," she muttered as she held Reagan tightly. Then she straightened her body and glared at Amanda. "With her!"

"She never betrayed you, Audie," Amanda said quietly. "She told me more than once that you were the love of her life. How lucky she was to have you. Please let me tell you the secret she couldn't."

Suddenly the sky rumbled, and fat raindrops began falling. "Perhaps we should go inside," Reagan suggested, quickly picking up their dinner plates. Amanda carried their glasses in behind her, while Audie closed the grill.

"There's supposed to be a small storm blowing in off the Gulf tonight," Amanda said, setting the glasses on the kitchen counter.

"Please find a seat, Amanda. I'll put some coffee on." Reagan smiled.

Amanda went into the main room and sat on a comfortable chair facing Audie, who sat on a teal Early American sofa, scowling.

Fifteen minutes later, Reagan brought three cups, creamer, and sugar, then poured the coffee into the cups. "I hope you like your coffee a little bold," she said. "It's all we have, apparently."

"The bolder, the better," Amanda said, taking a sip and nodding. "It's excellent. Thanks," she said and took another sip. "Get comfortable. This might take a while because I have to include a little background information about myself for it to make sense."

Audie prepared her coffee and snapped, "Just get on with this...fairy tale."

"Audie, please," Reagan chided gently.

Amanda took a deep breath and leaned back in her chair. "You're exactly the way Carlie described you." She smiled as she looked at Audie. "And Carlie was the woman you believed she was, so don't think poorly about her. She never cheated with me or anyone else. She loved you but couldn't bring herself to tell you about me." Amanda took a deep breath before beginning again. "I was adopted by a very sweet couple in Colorado. They chose to tell me I was adopted after I turned eighteen, but it didn't matter all that much to me at the time. They loved me unconditionally, but I'd always known I was different, just didn't know why. I only knew that I didn't look like either of my parents or my sister, who was born a couple of years after they adopted me."

"Lucky you," Audie groused impatiently.

"Yeah, I was extremely lucky. After I graduated from high school, I elected to go to culinary school rather than a university. During that time, I had a classmate who was also adopted. Unfortunately, he had several medical problems and searched for his birth parents for years to find out their medical history. He suggested I do the same so I'd at least be aware of any genetic problems that might pop up in the future. I discussed it with my mom and dad, and they both agreed it was a good idea, even though I'd never had an illness other than those that most children get. All they could tell me was where I was adopted. My folks hired an attorney, who eventually managed to have my adoption records unsealed."

"So, you were born in Colorado?" Audie asked skeptically.

"Yes. In Golden, Colorado." Amanda nodded.

Audie grinned. "Then that settles it. Carlie never went to Colorado in her life. Even refused to go when I suggested going for a ski trip. End of story."

"You might want to talk to Lynn to verify that," Amanda suggested.

"Who's Lynn?" Reagan asked.

"My wife's younger sister," Audie answered.

"I've never met her, but would like to someday," Amanda said and sighed. "But she *knows* Carlie was in Colorado from the fall of 1990 to the spring of 1991."

"Ridiculous," Audie said and sniffed.

"Anyway, when my record was unsealed, I saw my original birth certificate. I'm only referred to as Baby Carlson, but it clearly listed Cara Carlson as my birth mother and her home of record as Fredericksburg, Texas. Is that her hometown?"

Audie nodded glumly.

"No father was listed, so we hired a private investigator, and he tracked Carlie to Austin. He gave me her business address and her phone number. I wrote her a few times, but she never responded, so I finally decided to call her to at least get my father's name. After we spoke, she told me she was sorry, but couldn't give me a name and had no desire to either speak to me again or to meet me. It broke my heart, but she assured me she had no genetic problems I should be aware of. Despite her rebuff, I continued to send her letters. I even drove to Austin once and showed up at her business unannounced. I figured she might not have wanted me, but she was going to know that my life was a happy one, in case she'd worried about it.

"Finally, my sister, who was in college, talked me into driving down here with her for spring break about eight years ago. We discovered an old place in Port Aransas that was for sale. On a whim, I bought it and moved. It wasn't long after that Carlie agreed to meet me on the island for the first time. I was scared to death, but it seemed like I'd known her forever when we met. She was nervous, of course, but very warm and welcoming."

"She always was," Audie said. "I was just a small-town hick when we met, but I fell in love with her immediately. She had a way of putting people at ease. Why wouldn't she tell me any of this?"

"Maybe she was afraid to, thinking she might lose you if you knew," Reagan said.

"Or maybe she was ashamed of what she did," Amanda said.

"Nothing could have made me leave her," Audie said, shaking her head. "She was everything to me."

"Can you tell me how she died?" Amanda asked. "I know it must have been painful for you."

"She was diagnosed with breast cancer about four years ago, and like cancer usually does, it gradually robbed her of the life she knew and who she was. The last six months were the worst, and she just seemed to give up and wither away a little each day."

"I wish I'd known. I would have gladly driven to Austin to

help you care for her," Amanda said.

"She wouldn't have wanted that," Audie said and sighed. "She didn't want anyone to see her like that. She wouldn't even let Lynn or her parents visit us. It was a rough time," she said, wiping her eyes.

"So, you believe me then?" Amanda asked hopefully.

"I believe she came to love you, but I want to speak to Lynn and my in-laws after I get home. If true, it's a lot to process."

Amanda glanced at the clock hanging on the wall. "Damn, I have to get up in a few hours to begin prepping for tomorrow...or rather, today. If you're going to be here for another day or two, drop by the restaurant for a meal. My treat," she said and stood. "Thanks for listening to me." She hugged Audie hesitantly. "My mother was a lucky woman to have had you by her side," Amanda whispered.

"It was a pleasure meeting you, Reagan," she added, shaking her hand.

They escorted Amanda to the deck doors and waited until she drove away. Reagan slipped her arm around Audie's waist as they turned to re-enter the bungalow. "Feel better?"

"Some," Audie said and shrugged. "But I still want to talk to Lynn and Carlie's folks. Then maybe I'll know the whole truth." She locked the French doors and dropped onto the sofa. Looking at Reagan, she said, "She's only two years younger than you, you know."

"So what?" Reagan shrugged.

"I'm forty-five, walking all over forty-six," Audie said flatly. "That girl could have been *my* daughter. Doesn't that bother you?"

"Why would it?"

"Don't get the wrong idea, Reagan. You're a beautiful young woman. And you make me feel things I wouldn't have believed were possible again, but realistically there may be too many differences between us."

"Are you afraid of what your friends will think or say?" Reagan asked with a grin.

"No, but maybe you should be," Audie said, returning the smile.

"I don't let my friends dictate how I live or who I choose

to date."

"I'm not suggesting that you do. But your friends will talk, Reagan. My friends will mostly be jealous, but—"

Reagan reached down and stroked Audie's face. "Poor Audie. So strong, yet still so insecure and distrusting. I enjoy being with people who interest me, and you *fascinate* me. Younger women are too eager, and I'm not interested in anyone on a respirator. So, that makes you just about perfect. I think, at the very least, we could enjoy one another's company."

"Just be close friends, huh?" Audie grinned.

"The closer the better." Reagan breathed as she leaned down closer to Audie.

Audie reached up and slid her hand into the hair along the back of Reagan's neck, drawing her slowly into a hungry, possessive kiss. When their lips broke for a breath, Reagan leaned her forehead against Audie's and laughed. "Now *that's* what I'm talkin' about, baby."

****

Audie blinked her eyes open and ran a hand over her face, seeing shafts of bright sunlight streaming through the wooden plantation blinds covering the bedroom windows. She felt refreshed, smiling at the sight of the disheveled mass of light hair that spread over her chest. One of Reagan's arms draped possessively across Audie's waist, and her leg rested comfortably over Audie's thighs. She brushed her hand over Reagan's hair as she remembered the night before, the silky feel of Reagan's smooth skin sliding beneath her fingers and the incredible reaction of her own body every time Reagan touched her.

She couldn't believe anyone could make her feel that way again.

"Gawd. Who knew you would be such an animal in bed?" Reagan mumbled drowsily against Audie's chest. Audie sucked in a breath as Reagan's lips encircled a nipple and tugged gently. She sighed contentedly as she released Audie's nipple, pushed her hair back, and propped her head on her hand with a lazy smile. "But it was everything I could have hoped for and well worth not rushing into."

"Did I hurt you?" Audie asked, reaching out to stroke Reagan's cheek with the backs of her fingers. "I'm a little out of practice, so if I was too aggressive, I'm sorry."

Reagan laughed and leaned over to kiss Audie deeply. "You rocked my world last night, baby, but any time you think you need more practice, I'm absolutely available," she whispered, playfully nipping at Audie's chin. "But right now, I'm starving and must have sustenance."

"I can make ham and cheese omelets."

"Now you're talking. I'll even help by making toast and coffee," Reagan said, jumping out of bed. "Then I'd love to take another leisurely stroll along the beach."

Even though she was smiling as her eyes drank in the sight of Reagan's supple, naked body, Audie said, "I'm not complaining, but unless you're planning to eat breakfast and traipse down the beach buck naked, you might want to get dressed." She rolled out of the bed and pulled on a T-shirt and her boxers before squeezing Reagan's firm, smooth butt on her way to the kitchen.

****

Audie made the omelets while Reagan took care of the toast and coffee. Reagan made quick work of her food.

"This is a great omelet, Audie," Reagan said around a mouthful of food. "Will you teach me how to make these? I'm a barely adequate cook," she said, chewing another huge bite.

"Any time." Audie nodded and swallowed the food in her mouth, washing it down with a swig of her coffee. She cleared her throat and said, "I thought that after our walk on the beach, we might drive into Port Aransas. There are several galleries in town you might like. A few are a little touristy, but some are more upscale."

"Depending on how much time we spend looking, we could stop for an early dinner at Amanda's," Reagan suggested, stuffing the last bite of her omelet into her mouth.

"We don't have to. I think she's already told me everything she knows."

"Does she look like your wife?" Reagan asked, sipping her coffee.

"Yes. Her hair…and her eyes." Audie swallowed hard.

"Maybe after you speak to your sister-in-law and her parents, we can have a little get-together to introduce them to Amanda."

"Depending on what happened, they might not be interested in meeting her. After all, they apparently shipped Carlie off to another state before the kid was born," Audie said, clenching her teeth.

"Why didn't you and Carlie have any children?" Reagan asked casually as she drew her legs up against her chest and nibbled on her toast.

"I would have liked that, but Carlie didn't want children and refused to discuss adopting. Now I know why. Why all the questions, Reagan?" Audie asked, beginning to feel slightly uncomfortable.

Reagan shrugged. "I guess I'm just curious about the person you lived with, and loved, for so many years."

"Isn't that what most people do when they're in love? Besides, we put so much effort into getting our businesses off the ground and renovating our home and this place, we decided we had too much on our plates to start a family. But now I think she didn't want kids because it would have reminded her of what she'd already given up. Adopting would have reminded her every day of what she'd done, and she couldn't face that," Audie continued, rubbing her forehead.

"How did you meet?"

Audie smiled. "We met in college at a jock party. She was the most beautiful girl I'd ever met. I was pretty awkward and unsophisticated, but I worked up the guts to ask her out anyway. She was kind and funny and could always put me at ease." Glancing across the table, she admitted, "She was the only woman I ever wanted to sleep with…until last night."

Reagan blushed slightly. "Then I'm honored," she said quietly. She reached across the table and covered Audie's hand with her own, catching her eyes and smiling. "Truly," she added, squeezing Audie's hand lightly.

"Ready for that walk?" Audie asked as she stood and began clearing the table. "That little storm last night may have deposited a few good shells on the beach."

Chapter Ten

"Do you have any pictures of your work on your cell?" Audie asked as she helped Reagan from her vehicle.

"A few, why?" Reagan asked.

Audie shrugged. "Thought you might show them to a few gallery owners while we're here. Get a feel for their interest."

"I've been thinking about an idea for a new piece, inspired by what I've seen down here," Reagan said and grinned. "Now I'm anxious to get home and work on it, but it's only an idea at the moment," she said, taking Audie's hand and stepping out of the car.

Audie continued to hold her hand as they walked toward Gulf Coast Gallery, one of a group of stores located in a cul-de-sac shopping area off the main center. "Pick up something with each gallery's name and address on it," Audie whispered as they entered Gulf Coast Gallery. "If your new piece turns out the way you want, you can always email them a picture."

"Good idea," Reagan whispered back.

"Just a habit I learned from Carlie. We had boxes of business cards, brochures, and such. She never knew what might be useful in her business."

"What did she do for a living?"

"She owned a small but reasonably successful advertising and promotion company," Audie answered, placing her hand on Reagan's back as they wandered leisurely around the gallery.

After trooping through several other galleries and purchasing a couple small souvenirs, Audie drove to The Beachcomber's Inn and escorted Reagan inside. The same young woman stood behind the reception desk. She smiled broadly when she saw Audie. "Ms. Wade, it's nice to see you again."

Audie glanced around, noticing virtually every table was taken. "Thanks...uh...I'm sorry, but I didn't catch your name when I was here yesterday."

The woman extended her hand. "I'm Christina Lange, co-owner, Amanda's sister, and official greeter." She chuckled pleasantly. Then she suddenly frowned. "I was so sorry to learn that Carlie had passed away. Amanda told me this morning. She was the sweetest lady. I was so excited when she agreed to meet Amanda. We both loved her."

"Thank you. Did you see her often?"

Christina thought for a moment. "She drove down about once every couple of months for almost two years, then suddenly, four years ago, she told us she wouldn't be coming back and asked Amanda not to contact her again. Said it was because of a personal matter. Amanda was heartbroken."

"That was around the time her doctor diagnosed her with breast cancer," Audie said. "I'm sorry she chose to abandon Amanda...again."

Audie was tongue-tied momentarily before Reagan stepped forward with her hand out. "I'm Reagan Malloy, a friend of Audie's. Looks like you're pretty busy this afternoon."

"If you're here for an early dinner, you can either wait at the bar until a table opens up, or we can serve you at a booth in the bar area. Either way, Amanda will be thrilled to see you again," Christina said cheerfully.

"I don't mind eating in the bar if you don't," Reagan said, looking at Audie.

"I'm hungry, so I don't care either, and I wouldn't mind a drink first to relax," Audie said, taking Reagan's hand again as Christina led them to a booth a little away from the bar itself.

"I'll send a waitress over and let Amanda know you're here," Christina said. "Enjoy your meal."

A few minutes later, Amanda strode briskly to the booth as Audie and Reagan sipped their drinks. She leaned down to embrace each woman warmly, then brought a chair over to sit with them.

"Have you recovered from last night yet?" Amanda asked.

Audie looked at Reagan and grinned. "We had a very restful night's sleep. Must've been because of the storm. How about you?"

"I was so wired when I got home that I drank a pot of coffee and decided to drive down to the pier to greet the fishing and shrimp boats as they came in. So, our seafood is super fresh today," Amanda said and laughed. "I'll be draggin' by the time we close though."

"How's the lobster?" Reagan asked.

"Primo," Amanda answered. "I can personally recommend the Surf 'n Turf."

"Two of those with a garden salad sounds good," Audie said. "But I'll pay for our meals."

"I told you it would be my treat," Amanda protested.

"That's fine for grilled chicken or something else less expensive, but not this time, kiddo," Audie insisted. "Besides, I think Reagan likes it down here, so I'm sure we'll be back again."

"I hope so. I don't want to lose touch," Amanda said.

"You won't. I promise. Do you have a pen?" Audie asked.

Amanda stuck a hand into the pocket of her apron and fished out a ball-point pen. Audie grabbed a cocktail napkin and jotted down her home address and phone number. "And this is my office number. Feel free to contact me any time," Audie said, sliding the napkin to Amanda.

"Thanks. I can't tell you how glad I am to have finally met you, Audie," Amanda said. "I hope one day you'll be willing to tell me more about Carlie. You knew her better than anyone."

"I thought I did," Audie said sadly.

"Oh no, you knew the *most* important things. What she was like, what she enjoyed, her favorite way to spend her free time, what made her laugh or cry, those small things that were her life. That's what's important for me, to know about the woman who was my mother. I want to know who she was inside."

"I'd like to know more about her too, when you're ready," Reagan said, covering Audie's hand with her own. "You loved her."

Audie took in a deep breath and released it slowly. "We're going home tomorrow, but I swear the next time we come down, I'll tell you everything I can about Carlie. I wish we could stay longer, but work calls, for both of us. Let me talk to Lynn and Carlie's parents to organize their story first. Maybe that will make the whole story more complete."

****

A little after lunch the next day, Audie loaded their luggage into the back of her Subaru. She opened the rear passenger door and whistled for Buck, who ran around the side of the bungalow and leaped eagerly onto the seat. Then Audie did one last sweep through the bungalow before she locked up and headed outside to look for Reagan.

She located her seated on a small dune below the house, staring out over the Gulf, a light breeze blowing through her hair. Audie sat beside Reagan and wrapped an arm around her shoulders.

"I like it here, Audie," Reagan said, leaning against her. "I grew up in Houston, but it's not the same. It's so peaceful and...mind-freeing here. Thank you for bringing me."

"We'll be back," Audie said and kissed Reagan's temple. "I promise." Then Audie stood and pulled Reagan up. Reagan stumbled slightly as the sand on the dune gave way under her feet. Audie quickly reached out and grabbed her to prevent her from falling.

"Good catch." Reagan chuckled as she clung to Audie. Reagan pressed her body against Audie's for a moment. Looking up at Audie, she said, "I love the way you feel, so solid." Then she drew Audie down and explored her mouth with a solid kiss.

"Are you really that anxious to get back home?" Reagan teased while working her hands beneath Audie's shirt to tickle the skin on her abdomen. Audie jumped slightly, then held Reagan as she lowered her onto the sand.

"Thank you," Audie whispered while nuzzling Reagan's neck.

"For what?" Reagan laughed.

"For keeping me grounded when I heard the truth. It freed me." Audie hovered over Reagan and lowered her body to kiss her lightly. "Thank you," she repeated before kissing Reagan again. "Thank you," she said a third time. Finally, she kissed Reagan firmly and rolled over, pulling her on top of her body.

"You don't need to keep thanking me, baby," Reagan said softly. "But feel free to keep doing what you're doing," she said and grinned. "For as long as you want."

****

Three hours later, Audie pulled into Reagan's driveway. She carried Reagan's luggage inside, along with an assortment of things she'd picked up during their stay on Mustang Island. Once everything was unloaded and settled in the house, Reagan took Audie's hand and walked her to the front porch. "Be careful driving home," she said, running her hand down Audie's chest.

"I will, but I plan to stop at Lynn's for a few minutes first," Audie said.

"Are you going to tell her you met Amanda?"

Audie nodded. "They've kept that secret buried too damn long already. I loved Carlie, but now I feel like I never truly *knew* her."

Reagan cupped Audie's face in her hands and searched her eyes. "I think the thought of losing you terrified her. Many women wouldn't have been able to live with the choices she made. I believe Carlie loved you but didn't want to take a chance on losing you."

"I hate that she thought she couldn't trust me," Audie said, shaking her head slightly. "It hurts because she should have known better."

"I hope you find the answers you're looking for. Just try to keep an open mind," Reagan whispered.

Audie took Reagan by the shoulders. "Promise me you'll never lie to me...about anything."

"I can't promise that, Audie, and neither can you. We don't know what will happen in the future that we may want to deny or keep secret. The truth for me right now is that I'm beginning to care about you a lot and don't want anything to hurt you."

"I care about you too, Reagan, and, truthfully, the idea scares the hell out of me," Audie said and smiled.

"I'll miss you next to me tonight, baby. Was kinda gettin' used to wakin' up and seein' you beside me. Call me before you go to bed? I'll probably be up late anyway."

"Stop talking, sweetie, before I drag you back inside." Audie laughed. Then she ran her hands around Reagan's waist, pulled her closer, and kissed her thoroughly. Without thought, she moved her hands up Reagan's body until they cupped her breasts; her thumbs lightly stroked over the nipples and elicited a groan as Reagan pressed against Audie's hands.

"Oh...God, I love the way you touch me," Reagan said between breaths.

"I like touching you," Audie said. "But—"

"I know, you need to go and finish your search for the truth." Reagan sighed as she took Audie's hand. They walked to Audie's vehicle, and Reagan leaned down to kiss her one last time. "Call me later, okay?"

"Okay," Audie said before backing out of the driveway.

****

Audie trotted up the front steps of Lynn and Jerry Peterson's house and rang the doorbell. She heard the chimes inside, followed by footsteps. She smiled when Jerry opened the front door and pushed the glass storm screen door open. "Hey, Audie!" he exclaimed. "Good to see you again. Been a while." Then he called over his shoulder, "Babe, Audie's here!"

Lynn rushed out of the kitchen wiping her hands on her apron and hugged Audie tightly. "We just finished dinner. Would you like a bowl of chili?"

"Sounds good, Lynn. Thanks," Audie said and smiled.

"Then come on in the kitchen, honey. How are you?" Lynn chattered as she led Audie into the kitchen, filling a bowl with steaming chili.

"Actually, I just got back in town. I spent the weekend on the coast," Audie said quietly as she dug into her bowl. "Damn, Lynn, why didn't you ever teach me how to make this?" she said and smiled.

"Wouldn't have done you any good. You know Carlie hated chili," Lynn said and laughed.

"Never understood that. That's practically un-Texan, isn't it?"

"Everyone has different tastes, I guess. I'm not a fan of guacamole myself. There must be something you're not crazy about either."

"I'm not fond of lies and family secrets," Audie said seriously.

"Don't think I've ever had that," Lynn said with a smile.

"I met Amanda Lange while I was at the coast this weekend," Audie said calmly. "She was Carlie's secret, wasn't she? I know you knew about her, but you let me believe she was Carlie's lover when you *knew* she was Carlie's daughter. Why didn't you just tell me, Lynn?" She slapped her hand on the table. "I was ready to kill that sweet girl." Then she buried her head in her hands. "God, she looks so much like Carlie when she was the same age."

"Carlie didn't want you to know. She made me promise to never tell you. I was honoring her wishes and kept her secret. But I should have known you'd ferret it out, especially after you found that damn picture. I'm sorry, Audie."

"Is that why she didn't want to have children?"

Lynn shrugged. "I don't know. That was a difficult time for her, but maybe. Why?"

"How did she get pregnant and why did your folks ship her off to Colorado? She told me she knew she preferred girls by the time she was thirteen."

"I honestly don't know that part of the story, Audie. We never discussed it."

"Then call Don and Betty and get them over here," Audie insisted. "Everything about this little family secret needs to see the light of day. It's time, Lynn, so we can all move on."

****

"Lynn, do you have anything I can feed Buck while we wait? He's in my car, and I'm sure he's starving," Audie said after Lynn completed her call to her parents.

"Of course," Lynn said. "Bring him in, and I'll cook up some ground beef for him."

Audie went to her car and clipped a leash to Buck's collar, then led him back into Lynn's house where he gulped down a bowl of cooked ground beef followed by half a bowl of water. Then Audie turned him out into Lynn's backyard to run around. Audie, Lynn, and Jerry sat together leisurely in the den and killed time chatting and catching up until the chimes sounded. Lynn opened the front door and escorted her parents into the den.

"Bucky-boy," Don Carlson said with a smile as Buck was let back inside and jumped up to greet Carlie's father. Then he sat politely while Betty Carlson scratched his ears. "Good to see you again, Audie," Don said, patting her on the back. Betty embraced Audie warmly before everyone was seated again.

Finally, Lynn addressed her parents. "Audie has a couple of questions about Carlie she'd like to ask you, and I couldn't help her."

Betty looked at Audie and said, "You probably knew her as well as we did, dear, so I don't know what we can tell you now."

Audie frowned. "I thought I knew everything about her, too, but apparently I was wrong. As I told Lynn earlier, I drove to our place on the coast over the weekend. While I was there, I met a young woman named Amanda Lange, who told me a very interesting story. At first I was sure she was lying, but she finally convinced me it was the truth."

Betty looked at Don. "I don't think we know anyone by that name. Do you, honey?"

Don shook his head. "The name's not familiar. What about her?" he asked, looking at Audie.

"After Carlie...died," Audie started as her throat tightened, "while I was looking through her things, I read her journals. Several times, she mentioned someone named Amanda Lange, and it made me curious. And frankly, it sounded to me like Carlie was having an affair with her," she said bluntly and saw the looks of disbelief on her in-laws' faces. "Based on what I'd read in the journals, it sounded like she'd cheated on me when I was out of town on business."

"She would never!" Don said forcefully.

"She loved you, Audie," Betty said sternly.

"I know she did, but she didn't trust me enough to tell me the truth about Amanda Lange and their connection. I hired an investigator to locate her and drove to the coast to confront her over the weekend, and what I discovered shocked the hell out of me. To understand what I've already learned, I need to know why you sent Carlie to Colorado."

"She wanted to go," Betty said without looking at Audie.

"The St. Ignatius Academy for Girls had an excellent reputation."

Audie glanced at Don and Betty for a moment before finally asking, "Carlie was pregnant when you sent her there, wasn't she?"

Don took Betty's hand and looked at Audie. "Yes, she was. So, we decided to send her to Colorado to a private boarding school. Fredericksburg was a smaller, less sophisticated town back then, and it would have been difficult for her to remain there while she was pregnant. She refused to agree to an abortion."

"She was only fifteen," Betty said. "She went to a graduation party with some friends, and someone put something into her drink as a joke. An older boy raped her while she was unconscious."

"Oh, my God," Audie muttered.

"Two or three months later, when Don and I discovered she was pregnant, we transferred her to St. Ignatius to protect her. She stayed there until the baby was born. Then we transferred her back to Fredericksburg to complete high school and never spoke about it again."

"Well, that baby grew up, and her name is Amanda Lange," Audie said, withdrawing a photo from her jacket pocket. "She's a lovely, accomplished young woman that Carlie eventually grew very close to. Who was the father?"

"We never knew for sure, but Carlie eventually came to believe it was a boy, a senior, named Travis Downs. Apparently, while he was drinking at another party, he bragged about what he had done to her to some of his friends, but later denied it," Betty said.

"Does he still live in Fredericksburg?" Audie asked.

"His family does," Don said. "But Travis was killed driving home from A&M near the end of his first semester."

"He was drunk," Betty spat.

"Why didn't she just tell me? I loved her," Audie said. "I wouldn't have cared or loved her any less."

"She was so ashamed, even though we both assured her it wasn't her fault. I'd have beat that fool to death if I'd gotten my hands on him," Don snarled angrily.

Betty took the picture from Audie, and she and Don stared

at it. "She looks so much like Carlie when she was younger," Betty said with a sniff.

"Where the hell was I when all this was going on?" Lynn asked.

"Off doing whatever ten-year-old girls do, I suppose," Don said, smiling at her fondly.

"Where is Amanda now?" Betty asked.

"She and her sister live in Port Aransas. They opened an excellent restaurant there," Audie said and smiled.

"I'm not sure about Don, but I'd like to meet her," Betty said.

"I'm sure she'd want that, too, Betty. Just give her a little time first. I had to tell her Carlie had passed away, which was the reason Carlie suddenly stepped out of her life for the second time about three years ago," Audie explained. Then she stood and said, "It was good to see you both again, Don, Betty, but right now, I'm exhausted and need to head home."

"Wait a sec, Audie," Lynn said and stood up. "Let me put some of my chili into a container for you."

When Lynn hustled off to the kitchen, Don and Betty stood. Betty, a relatively short woman, pulled Audie down and threw her arms around Audie's neck, hugging her tightly. "My daughter loved you, Audie. Don't ever forget that."

"I won't, Betty, but I'm sorry Carlie didn't feel secure enough to tell me about Amanda."

"Try not to judge her," Don added when he leaned forward and squeezed Audie's shoulder.

"I loved Carlie. We could have been a family," Audie said.

"You...we still can be, sweetie," Betty said and sniffed.

"Amanda wants to know everything about Carlie. You'll all have to help me with that," Audie added, accepting a large container of chili from Lynn.

Audie snapped her fingers. "Let's go home, Buck."

After getting in her car, Audie thought about what she'd learned from her in-laws, still wishing Carlie had trusted her enough to tell her what had happened to her as a young girl. It wouldn't have caused Audie to love her less, and they might have had the family she'd always wanted. She was determined to make Carlie's daughter a part of her family now...somehow.

****

Audie was tired when she arrived home, but she'd promised to call Reagan. After letting Buck into the backyard, she sank down onto the couch and dialed Reagan's number, tilting her head against the back of the couch.

"Hi, baby," Reagan's breathless voice answered after the second ring.

"Hi, sweetie," Audie responded. "Sorry it's kind of late. What were you doing?"

"Getting ready for bed," Reagan said in a low, seductive voice.

"Wish I was there to see that," Audie flirted.

"Use your imagination, Audie. You've watched me get ready for bed once or twice," Reagan said and laughed.

Audie smiled at the memory. "I have, but I seem to remember you were naked at the time. Now I have to imagine touching you. It's not quite as…satisfying. I miss you," she admitted.

"What are you doing?"

"Relaxing on the couch. Imagining that I'm kissing you and how good you feel against me," Audie teased.

"Stop, Audie, or I'm going to come," Reagan groaned.

"Promise?" Audie asked. "You look so beautiful and free when you come, baby."

"Did you find out everything you wanted to know from your in-laws?"

"I learned everything that mattered. I'll tell you tomorrow. Thought I might take you out to dinner at The Driskill Grill. They have great steaks."

"Would you like to come back over tonight?"

"Nothing I'd enjoy more, but Suzanne and I have an early video conference with a potential new client tomorrow morning. Depending on how that goes, we'll be flying to Knoxville on Wednesday or Thursday, so, I'll see you tomorrow evening…about seven. Sleep well," Audie said.

"You too, baby," Reagan whispered and ended the call.

****

Audie held Reagan's hand as she walked her to her front door after dinner the next night.

"Come in for a drink before you go home?" Reagan asked.

"Maybe just a small one," Audie said and smiled. "I still need to pack."

Audie helped Reagan remove her coat, brushing her hair aside to kiss the side of her neck. Reagan hummed before twirling around and covering Audie's lips with an inviting kiss that lingered as Audie pressed Reagan against her. She couldn't stop her hands from slipping beneath Reagan's blouse, the fullness of her breasts filling Audie's palms. When their lips parted, Audie panted. "I think I could really use that drink now, before I get any more carried away."

"Feel free to let yourself get carried away," Reagan breathed, finding Audie's lips again and kissing her passionately. "Do you have a clue how much I want you, baby?" she added, taking Audie's bottom lip between her teeth.

"I want you too, Reagan," Audie whispered. "You don't know how much or what you do to me."

"Make yourself comfortable while I get our drinks," Reagan said, kissing Audie lightly.

Audie took her time glancing around Reagan's living room. She spotted a few framed photographs on a bookcase and wandered over to examine them more closely. She picked up one of Reagan with her arms around a young woman as they looked at one another. Even in profile, the woman looked vaguely familiar. While she was staring at the picture, her eyes were drawn to the matting surrounding the photo. It was ornately calligraphied with names and the date it was taken. Audie frowned, certain she recognized the writing.

From behind her, Reagan said, "That's me with my best friend, Emily. When we went to Dickens on the Strand in Galveston three or four years ago. That's where we got matching tattoos around our arms after a drink or two too many. We thought they would make us look cool and tough, but we both cried like babies." She chuckled at the memory.

"Pretty girl," Audie said and studied the photograph once more. "Interesting matting," she said before setting the picture back on the bookshelf.

"Tracey took the picture and did the mat for me so I wouldn't forget where we were or how happy Em seemed that day."

"You both look happy," Audie noted.

"I was feeling no pain, but Em was pretty much her usual unhappy self," Reagan said and sighed. "She suffered from problems with depression, which is probably why everyone thinks she killed herself," she said sadly. "But I'll never believe that. I just can't."

"I'm sorry," Audie said, taking her drink.

"Me, too," Reagan said and shrugged. "She spent most of her life searching for the happiness she longed for, believing she could find it by picking up total strangers in a bar who might make her feel better about herself," Reagan said forcefully.

"You sound angry," Audie said softly.

"I am angry, dammit," Reagan spat and covered her eyes with her hand. "Someone killed my friend and got away with it, and no one cares."

Audie set her drink down and took Reagan in her arms to soothe her, but she couldn't get the young woman's face out of her mind, trying unsuccessfully to remember where she might have seen her. "What can I do to help you, honey?" Audie mumbled.

"Nothing." Reagan sniffed, looking up at Audie with watery eyes. "But thank you for listening while I vented."

Audie took Reagan's face between her hands and offered a slight smile before kissing her softly. "My pleasure. Anytime." Glancing at her wristwatch, she sighed. "Unfortunately, I need to get home and throw a few things together for my trip tomorrow."

"Call me so I'll know you arrived safely?" Reagan asked as she embraced Audie. "I'm sorry, baby. This wasn't how I wanted the evening to end."

"Oh, really." Audie grinned, slipping her arm around Reagan's waist. "What did you have planned?"

"Something a little more...stimulating," Reagan said with a slight blush.

"Hold that thought. I'll be back in a couple of days and

promise to make it up to you." Audie smiled as she opened the front door slightly, stopping to indulge in a lingering kiss.

"Please don't leave, Audie. I need to feel your mouth on me again tonight," Reagan pleaded, burying her face on Audie's chest when their kiss ended. "And it'll be days before I see you again."

Audie kicked the door closed and sucked in a deep breath as Reagan took her hand and backed slowly toward her bedroom. She teased her bottom lip playfully with her teeth as her other hand began unbuttoning Audie's shirt.

****

Audie was sound asleep, her hand lazily resting in the valley between Reagan's breasts, when the sound of a car horn found its way into her subconscious and awakened her. She rubbed her face, and Reagan rolled over closely against her, running her hand over Audie's chest.

"What's wrong, baby?" Reagan mumbled sleepily.

"Sounds like some idiot accidentally set off their car alarm," Audie rasped. She sat up and glanced out the blinds next to the bed. "Shit! I think that's my car alarm.". Audie grabbed her shirt and pants and hopped around the bed, in an attempt to get dressed.

"Might've been a neighborhood stray cat walking on the hood," Reagan said as she flopped back down and ran a hand over her hair to push it away from her face.

"I'll check and turn the alarm off. Go back to sleep," Audie said while she felt around for her car keys and left the room.

Audie stepped onto the front porch and pressed the alarm button on her key fob. She smiled at the instant silence, then turned around to re-enter the house. She realized something seemed off. She cautiously moved down the front steps, looking around as she approached her vehicle, wishing she had a flashlight. She quickly went back up the porch steps, opened the front door, and reached in to flip on the porch light.

Once she could see the car, she realized all four tires were flat. The back window was shattered, and the brake and headlights were broken. Deep scratches were gouged into the paint of the front doors, but she couldn't tell if the scratches were words. A message on the windshield, in bright yellow paint, clearly read, *You were warned!*

Audie spotted a can of spray paint and bent over to pick it up.

While Audie was examining her vehicle, a patrol car pulled to the curb, and two police officers got out, drawing their weapons. "Step away from the vehicle and drop to your knees. Now!" one of the officers ordered as they approached Audie.

Audie raised her hands. "This is my car. Someone vandalized it. I was getting ready to call you."

"That why you're holding that can of spray paint?" the officer asked.

"It was lying next to my car," she said through clenched teeth as the second officer pulled her hands to her back and began handcuffing her. He then pulled her up and quickly frisked her. "No identification," he said.

"It's in the house. The car alarm woke me up, so I came out to check and saw the damage to my vehicle," Audie explained patiently.

"We received an anonymous call about someone vandalizing a vehicle at this address. And guess what, chief? We found you," the officer said and smirked.

Reagan, now awake and dressed, stepped out of the house as they were leading Audie toward their patrol car.

"Wait!" she called out. "What the hell are you doing?"

"I think they're arresting me for vandalizing my own damn vehicle. Find my wallet so I can identify myself, please. It should be on the dresser in the bedroom."

After checking Audie's ID and the vehicle registration in the glove compartment, they unlocked and removed her handcuffs and took a report. The officers advised Audie to take pictures of the damage, then contact her insurance carrier, and have the vehicle towed to a mechanic. Their report would be ready in a few days, and her insurance company could then send out an adjuster to look over the vehicle and give an estimate of the damages.

A little over an hour later, a tow truck from her Subaru dealership arrived to take the vehicle to their service department to await an adjuster.

"I liked that car," Audie said as they watched the tow truck roll away.

"What will you do now?" Reagan asked.

"Get dressed and call a cab, I guess. I'll have to let Suzanne know she'll be making our trip alone unless she wants to take Gia for company. Then I'll contact my insurance agent to see if my policy will pay for a rental car. I don't know how long it might take until they have it repaired."

"Why don't we try to get some sleep after you call Suzanne. I can drive you home after breakfast, honey," Reagan offered as she squeezed Audie tightly.

"Honestly, babe, I'm wide awake now. Would you mind making a pot of coffee while I wake up Suzanne and ruin her sleep, too?" Audie asked, dropping a kiss on Reagan's forehead.

"Sounds good to me," Reagan said with a smile before heading to the kitchen.

****

It was around ten the next morning when Reagan drove Audie home in her Volkswagen Beetle. She laughed as Audie tried to find a comfortable position for her long legs, but still ended up with her knees semi-folded against her chest. When Reagan pulled into the drive on the side of the house, it took Audie a few minutes to get her legs stretched out again.

"Buck's going to be pissed at me for leaving him home alone all night," Audie said as she unlocked the door from the garage into the kitchen.

"Hey, Audie," Reagan called out after meandering into the living room.

"What?"

"Looks like something broke several front windows. Did that happen before you came over yesterday?" Reagan asked as Audie joined her.

"They were fine when I left," Audie said, stepping into the wide front hallway entrance to examine the broken windows more carefully. Then she spun around. "Buck! Buck! Where are you, buddy?" she called out and whistled. "Check the bathroom, Reagan. He hides in there sometimes if he gets scared. I'll look in the kitchen."

As Reagan wandered down the main hallway, she heard whining. Her eyes widened when she saw what looked like blood smears on the tan tile floor leading down the length of the hallway.

"Audie!" she screamed. "Buck's hurt!"

Audie ran down the hall, and Reagan pointed at the blood. "Oh God, no!" Audie said, quickly following the trail of blood to her home office, the last room off the hallway. She fell to her knees next to her injured pet, stroking his broad head. "Don't die, buddy. Please don't die," she whispered as she buried her face in his fur. He gently licked her cheek. "Grab a towel from the bathroom and start your car," she snapped at Reagan. "We'll be there in a minute."

Reagan tossed Audie a large bath towel and ran to her small vehicle, praying there would be room for Audie and the injured animal in the back seat. Almost immediately, Audie stepped out of the kitchen and into the garage, holding Buck in her arms. She slid into the cramped back seat and pulled his head onto her lap while Reagan pushed his hind end as far onto the seat as she could before carefully closing the door.

"He's going to get blood on your seat back here. I'll pay to have it cleaned," Audie muttered.

"You think I give a damn about that right now?" Reagan exclaimed as adrenalin pumped through her body. "Just tell me where the hell we're going!"

"Try to calm down, Reagan. There's an animal hospital just off the Research Exit on the Loop. Go there," Audie instructed calmly. "It's going to be all right, Buck. Just a few more minutes, pal," she said softly.

As soon as Reagan brought her car to a screeching halt in front of Research Boulevard Animal Hospital, she jumped out and ran inside, returning less than a minute later with two vet techs. They gently picked Buck up and carried him inside while Reagan helped Audie out of the car. Audie's shirt was soaked with Buck's blood, but she didn't seem to notice as she followed Reagan into the waiting room.

A veterinary assistant came out half an hour later to get some information and tell Audie what the vet had discovered after a quick examination and an X-ray.

"He's lost quite a lot of blood, but apparently the bullet missed any vital organs," he said.

Audie grabbed his arm and said with a frown, "Bullet? You mean someone shot my dog? I thought he was cut by glass when someone broke out my front windows."

"The X-ray showed a clear bullet track. Fortunately, it was mostly soft tissue damage, and they're closing the wound in surgery. He should recover without issue. He might need to stay here for a couple of days because of the blood loss and to watch for possible infection," the assistant said. "Do you know how it happened?"

"No," Audie said, shaking her head. "I wasn't home last night."

"Probably a good thing," the assistant said, "or you could have been injured as well. We'll let you know when he's out of surgery."

Once they were alone again, Audie looked at Reagan. "Do you have your cell with you?"

"Yes," Reagan said and handed it to her.

Audie dialed the number for the police to report what had happened at her house. After giving her pertinent details, Reagan watched as Audie listened to whatever the person at the other end of the line said and then disconnected, handing the phone back to Reagan. "Thank you."

"You seem pretty calm, sweetie. Are you okay?" Reagan asked.

"When I find out who did it...I swear I'll kill them. Does that sound okay to you?" Audie answered tightly. "Even if Buck survives, whoever did this has no idea what they've taken from me," she added, burying her hands in her hair. "As soon as I know how...Buck is, I have to meet the police at the house."

Reagan ran a hand down Audie's back. "We'll figure it out, baby," she said softly.

****

By the time Reagan and Audie arrived back at Audie's house, a number of police officers were busy examining the area around the building and nearby grounds. An older man with graying hair and a suit jacket slung over his shoulder ambled toward Reagan's Beetle as she brought it to a stop in the drive. Audie opened the passenger door and unfolded her long legs to step out of the vehicle. The first thing she noticed were the man's cowboy boots as he greeted her and extended a hand to assist her out of the confining car. "Ms. Wade?" he asked.

When she nodded and shifted her eyes to her house, he said, "Sergeant Delbert Bowers, Property Crimes Division, ma'am. Sorry about the mess."

"Do you know anything yet?" Audie asked.

"Right now we know a neighbor called in a report about hearing gunfire last night, but not much else," Bowers said. "I'll need to ask you a few questions."

Audie nodded. "Of course. Please come inside." She unlocked the kitchen door and stepped in, waiting as Bowers and Reagan entered.

"Sorry it's not cooler in here, Sergeant," Audie said pleasantly, "but as you can see, the windows are letting in quite a bit of warm air. Can I offer you a bottle of cold water?"

"No, thanks," Bowers said as he located a chair and settled at the kitchen table.

"Do you want a bottle of water, honey?" Reagan asked, resting a hand on Audie's shoulder.

"Please," Audie said and sat across from Bowers.

"May I have your full name, please?" Bowers began his interview.

"Audra Elise Wade."

"Occupation?"

"I'm an attorney here in Austin," Audie said blandly.

"Any unhappy clients?"

"I specialize in contractual law, Sergeant, and am happy to say I don't usually have unhappy clients. My clients are primarily non-adversarial." Noticing the look on Bowers' face, she added, "In other words, we very rarely have to go into court," Audie said, attempting a smile.

"Any enemies you're aware of?" Bowers asked, flipping over a page in his notebook.

Audie shook her head. "None, but I suppose there may be

someone out there that I don't know about. I live a peaceful, sedate life, Sergeant. Or rather I have until recently."

"Are you doin' anything differently?"

Audie shrugged. "Wish I could tell you. But last night my car was vandalized, and when I came home this morning, I discovered my house, as well as my dog, had been shot up."

"I guess those two things could be a coincidence, but personally, I don't believe in coincidences, ma'am. Where is your car now?"

"I had it towed to Jenson Subaru. I have the towing receipt, if you need it," Audie offered.

"Is it registered in your name?"

"Yes."

A knock at the kitchen door halted the interview as Bowers stood to answer it, speaking a minute to a uniformed officer. When he returned, he said, "They found a place where they believe our shooter may have been lyin' in wait, probably waitin' for you to return home. It's possible gettin' your car vandalized could have saved your life inadvertently. Or it could have been a teenager tryin' out a birthday present or somethin'. But I guarantee we'll be checkin' out any possibilities. Don't hesitate to call if you think of anything else that might be useful."

"Thank you, Sergeant," Audie said and shook his hand. "Is it okay if I clean up some of this mess and make arrangements to have my windows replaced?"

"Yes, ma'am. We got what we needed in the house, but I think everything we were gonna find is outside."

After closing the front door, Audie entered the living room and looked around at the colored shards of glass that seemed to cover everything. She squatted down and picked up a fairly large piece of glass, then brought a hand up and covered her eyes.

Reagan was suddenly beside Audie, her arms wrapped securely around her as she sobbed. Audie wrapped her arms around Reagan and cried uncontrollably. "W...why? I d...don't understand," she hiccupped, trying to gather herself. "W...who have I h...hurt so much that th...they would...do this?" Then she stood up abruptly and grabbed her cellphone from her pocket. "I need to get someone over to replace my windows," she muttered as she dialed.

"Why don't you spend tonight at my place, sweetie?" Reagan asked as she joined Audie and ran a hand over her back.

"I need to get my life back under control," Audie snapped angrily.

"I know, babe, but maybe you should start on that after a good meal and a peaceful night's sleep," Reagan suggested.

Audie glared at Reagan and held up the piece of glass she'd picked up off the floor. "You don't have a clue what this meant to me, do you?" she demanded heatedly.

"It was obviously something important to you. I'm sorry, Audie."

Audie shook the fragment in front of Reagan's face and seethed. "This was part of the last anniversary gift Carlie gave me. She designed all of those now-shattered stained glass panels and commissioned an artist to make them for me," she said as her voice began to quiver while tears ran down her cheeks. "And now they're just...gone! Poof! Like they were nothing! Like it didn't matter! But Carlie mattered...*to me*. She was my everything and *always* will be," Audie said loudly as she fought against the tears and anger. "I'm sorry, Reagan, but that's *my* truth."

"I'm sorry, too, Audie. I honestly thought you were the one I've been searching for, but obviously you're still in love with another woman. I can't fight a ghost, and I *won't* be your back-up plaything for a memory you can never be with again. We both need some time and space to think, so I'm leaving now," Reagan said, with a sad tone of finality in her voice.

Audie watched her leave and cringed when the door slammed shut behind Reagan. She picked up her house phone and began calling businesses to have her windows replaced and to arrange to have a rental vehicle delivered. She also called the vet to check on Buck's condition and left a message on Suzanne's phone explaining she would not be at work for a few days. Lastly, she changed into her running clothes, hoping a strenuous run would help alleviate her rage, at least temporarily.

Without taking the time to do her ordinary stretch exercises, Audie launched into a full-out run, hearing nothing other than her running shoes slapping against the ground under her feet and her heart beating faster and faster.

She'd played under stress and handled it by knowing Carlie was in the stands cheering for her. She had handled the stress of establishing her business with Suzanne by knowing there was someone waiting for her at home at the end of a long day. But, as she kicked her pace up another notch, she realized that the events of the last couple of days had overwhelmed her, and she couldn't handle it because, for the first time, she was alone. Hell, she didn't even have Buck to accompany her on this impromptu run.

Her calves burned, but she pushed her body harder. Tears ran down her face, and she wiped them away angrily. The next time her left foot hit the ground, she grabbed the back of her leg, feeling her hamstring seize up, and fell to her knees. She managed to roll onto her back and suck in deep breaths to calm down.

Gradually, her heart rate slowed, and her mind cleared. What had she done? She was alone because of her inability to let her past go, to let Carlie leave peacefully, to allow someone else into her life. She'd thrown away a possible happy future by clinging to a past that would never be there to comfort her again. She needed to find a way to make Reagan believe how sorry she was. But first things first. She had to find a way to get back on her feet and drag her ass home, soak her leg, and wrap it.

She knew she'd screwed up her budding relationship with Reagan, possibly ending it completely. She needed to find a way to try to gain her forgiveness because, Audie admitted to herself, finally, that she cared for Reagan. No. She loved Reagan, and she refused to lose her—and lose her chance to live again.

****

Reagan managed to hold back her tears until she was sitting in her car. She lowered her head onto her hands, which tightly gripped her steering wheel, and gave in to her emotions. She cried all the way to her house and collapsed on her couch as soon as she got inside. As she tried to control her anger and sadness, her cell chirped, but when she glanced at the display, she noticed that the caller ID indicated it was Audie. She ignored the call and all the others over the next three hours, finally blocking Audie's number. She wasn't ready to speak to her again. Maybe she never would be prepared to speak to her again.

Finally, Reagan got up and changed into her old work jeans and a T-shirt and went to her workshop to do something that would take her mind off her problems. Within minutes, she was deep into her creativity.

Reagan was concentrating so much on her work that she didn't hear the door of the workshop open or close until she felt arms wrap around her waist. She spun around and yelled at the grinning woman behind her, "Jesus, Trace, I'm welding here and could've burned you! What the hell were you thinking?" Reagan turned off her torch and dropped it on the fire-resistant pad on her workbench.

She pulled off her welding mask and angrily threw it the length of her workshop before Tracey reached out and pulled Reagan into her arms, hugging her tightly. "I'm sorry, Trace, but the last day or so have been a little...rough," Reagan said, resting her head on Tracy's shoulder.

"What's wrong?" Tracey tightened her arms around Reagan, slowly rocking their bodies from side-to-side.

"Audie and I broke up this morning," Reagan said and sniffed.

"Maybe it's for the best, Reagan," Tracey said softly. "I don't know her very well, but she seemed a little too old for you anyway. Hey, you got a beer out here?"

"Yeah, in the fridge," Reagan said, stepping back and shoving her hands in the back pockets of her jeans. "Grab one for me, too, will ya?"

Tracey opened two beers and handed one to Reagan. "Feel like a thick, juicy steak tonight, babe? I'll provide the steak if you grill," Tracey said and smiled. "Sorta my treat."

Reagan frowned slightly at Tracey's use of "babe" but put it out of her mind quickly. She'd heard Tracey say something similar before, but this was the first time it bothered her. Reagan brushed it off, deciding it was just Tracey trying to cheer her up. "Well, I haven't eaten since last night, so I'm starving. I'd be willing to grill, if you fix the potatoes. I'll fire up the grill while you go get the steaks. And they better be prime rib thick," Reagan said with a smile.

"I'll be back in a flash," Tracey said, taking a deep swallow of her Longneck. She paused to look down at Reagan and impulsively dropped a kiss on her lips before walking to her motorcycle. Reagan touched her lips, wondering what the hell just happened.

****

Three days after the incident at her house, Audie sat behind her desk and rubbed her thumb and forefinger over her forehead. She'd read the same clause of the contract in front of her for the fourth time, but her mind wasn't engaging. She leaned back in her chair and closed her eyes. She knew she'd been angry, but she shouldn't have taken her anger out on Reagan. She was nothing but helpful after Audie discovered the damage to her home and Buck's injury.

She had no right to practically scream at Reagan because she lost it over a chunk of glass. Audie wasn't surprised that she couldn't concentrate on her job. She'd had little sleep, seemingly listening for any noise that might signal another attack. Her windows were replaced, and she was driving a rental car until hers was repaired.

She brought Buck home the previous day but had slept on a palette on the floor beside him to settle him down when he whimpered while he attempted to move into a more comfortable position. She called Suzanne and told her everything that happened, including what she'd said to Reagan. Audie cleaned up all the broken glass, scrubbed Buck's dried blood from the tiles on the floor, and patched the bullet holes in the wall opposite the front windows.

The next weekend she would paint the living room wall. She'd contacted the artist who'd made the glass panels. He still had the original patterns and promised he would be able to reproduce them, but it would take two or three months before he could deliver them. During their discussion, Audie made what she considered a brilliant decision.

She'd called Reagan several times each day, but her calls

were blocked. She kept trying, hoping against hope her call would go through. Though none ever did. How had everything gone so wrong so quickly?

"Taking a nap?" Suzanne asked with a laugh as she walked into Audie's office.

"No, just having a little trouble concentrating," Audie said, opening her eyes. "Do you need something, Suzanne?"

"Only playing mailman again," Suzanne said as she placed Audie's mail on her desk.

"Was your trip fruitful?" Audie flipped through her mail, tossing most of it into the trash can next to her desk.

"Fairly fruitful. Probably will need you to prepare four or five contracts as soon as I iron out a few sticky points. Shouldn't take long."

Audie picked up a No. 10 envelope with no return address that had her name written in the same calligraphied writing she'd received once before. She tore it open and pulled out a folded sheet of linen paper.

In large letters across the sheet were two lines: *Final warning! Stay away from her or the next time it won't be just your dog that bleeds!*

"What is it?" Suzanne asked.

"A fan letter, from someone who isn't really a fan." Audie handed the paper to Suzanne.

"This is a fuckin' threat! You need to call the police right now."

"I will, and I'll give them the first one I received, too." Audie nodded.

"When did this shit start?"

"After I first took Reagan out. Actually, I think someone really wants me to stop seeing her. First it was a note telling me to stay away from her. It's escalated from there. After we went to the retreat, I spent the night at her house, and my car was vandalized. She drove me home the next morning, and someone had shot out my front windows and shot Buck."

"If this guy is willing to vandalize your car and shoot up your home, he's already seriously unstable. Sounds more like he's got a hard-on for *you*."

"I'm not sure it's a guy. Reagan doesn't exactly hide her preference for women. She needs to be warned that she might be in danger, but she won't speak to me."

"Let the police do that, Audie."

"I will, but I need to apologize to her, too, and they can't do that. It has to be me."

"Why?" Suzanne asked, exasperated.

"Because I care about her." Audie shrugged.

"You care about Buck. Like that?"

"No. I care about her more than that," Audie said with a frown.

"Then why can't you just spit it out for God's sake?"

"I love her, okay. Does that make you happy?" Audie said loudly.

"More importantly, does it make *you* happy?"

"Extremely." Audie sighed.

"Then what's the problem?"

"I was upset after what happened at my house, and I yelled at her. I...I said Carlie was the only woman I ever loved or ever would."

"Well, that's a mood killer. What did she say then?"

"Nothing really. She said we needed some time and space, then walked out and won't talk to me. It was a stupid thing to say."

"Begging looks like your only option now, so I suggest you do that...soon."

****

It was slightly after five that evening when Audie pulled her rental car into the drive of Reagan's cozy home. She leaned against the headrest, attempting to organize her thoughts. A hundred ways of apologizing to Reagan for her unforgiveable outburst ran through her mind. All she could hope for was that Reagan would be willing to listen to her. She realized that putting it off any longer was pointless, so she finally opened the car door and stepped out, taking a minute to adjust and straighten her suit. She ran a hand through her hair and took a deep, steadying breath before making her way up the front steps.

The front door was open, and through the storm door, Audie could see Reagan lying on the sofa, her head resting in

Tracey's lap. Tracey's eyes were closed, but the fingers of one hand slowly stroked up and down Reagan's arm. After pushing her initial anger aside and composing herself, Audie rapped on the door. Reagan opened her eyes for a moment, then rolled over, turning her face into Tracy's abdomen. Tracey opened her eyes and glared at the door before carefully extricating herself from beneath Reagan's head. She walked quietly to the door and opened it a crack.

"I don't know if you remember me or not, but I'm Audie Wade, and I need to speak to Reagan," Audie said clearly.

"I *know* who you are," Tracey said derisively as her eyes scanned the length of Audie's tall body. "She doesn't want to speak to you, so beat it."

When Tracey started to close the door, Audie grabbed it to stop her. "I'd rather hear that from her. If she tells me to leave, I will, but she needs to listen to what I need to say."

"She's sleeping, but I'll tell her you stopped by. Maybe she'll call you later." Tracey frowned. "But I'm not gonna let you disturb her right now. So leave before I call the cops." She closed the door and locked it before Audie could react.

"Son of a bitch!" Audie shouted as her fist struck the wood next to the door. She spun around and stomped down the front steps to her car and drove away.

****

"Who was at the door?" Reagan mumbled when Tracey lifted her head and placed it back on her lap.

"Nobody important," Tracey said softly as she began lightly scratching Reagan's scalp. "Go back to sleep."

"I might have just been dozing, but I could have sworn I heard Audie's voice," Reagan said, turning onto her back and staring up at Tracey's frowning face.

"Probably just a nightmare." Tracey smiled down at her.

"Well, I need to get up anyway. I have things to do besides sleep my life away, although it was damn comfortable." Reagan yawned, stretching her arms over her head before forcing herself off the sofa. Glancing around, she asked, "Where's my cell phone?"

Tracey rummaged around on the end table next to her and

located the errant cell phone, handing it to Reagan, but withdrawing it teasingly every time Reagan reached for it. "Enough," Reagan finally said, grabbing it away from her.

"What's so important?" Tracey laughed.

"Well, since I apparently dreamed about hearing Audie, I thought I'd call to see how Buck is doing."

Tracey reached out and slapped the phone out of her hand.

"What the hell was that?"

"You told me you broke up with her," Tracey ground out.

"I did, but after having a few days to think about it, I think she was just stressed out after everything that was happening. First her car was vandalized, and then her house was shot up by some psycho, injuring her pet and destroying some things that meant a lot to her. How would you feel if someone trashed your bike, then tore up your house, and you had no idea why?" Reagan's voice rose as she spoke. When she finally stopped talking, she reached out and rested her hand against Tracey's chest, adding wistfully, "Plus I miss her…a lot. I miss the way she touched me."

"What the fuck is wrong with you, Reagan? Why are you pining away for someone who treated you like a dog when someone who loves you is standing right in front of you? I've loved you since middle school, but you've never bothered to look at me twice."

"Because you're my friend, Trace." Reagan backed up a step, shocked by Tracey's declaration.

"Emily was your *friend*, but I know you fucked her! Why not me? I've given you everything. If that fuckin' mutt had just stopped its damn yappin', it wouldn't have gotten hurt. Everything else was only stuff that didn't mean shit!"

"You shot Audie's dog?" Reagan asked, incredulous. "Why would you do that? Are you out of your mind?"

"Because I was losing you…again. You wasted your time on that loser, Emily. Then once she was gone, you took up with someone else who wasn't good enough for you and didn't deserve you. I'm the only one you can trust to protect you. Don't you understand that?" Tracey jerked her cell from the back pocket of her jeans and punched a few buttons before jamming it in Reagan's face.

"What the hell is this?" Reagan asked, pushing it away.

"Proof of what Emily was doing behind your back and the last woman she fucked. Enlarge it and you'll see your precious Emily with your newest heart-throb." When Reagan hesitated, Tracey yelled, "Look at it, dammit!"

Reagan enlarged the picture on Tracey's cell and couldn't deny it was Audie, leaning down to kiss Emily as she guided her into a motel room. The time and date stamp on the photo confirmed it had been taken the night before Emily died. Suddenly, Reagan felt sick. She ran into the bathroom to splash cold water on her face until her stomach settled down enough to allow her to return to the living room.

"Were you following Emily? You told me after her funeral that you didn't have time to go out clubbing with her."

Tracey shrugged. "I thought I might be able to talk her out of picking up another stranger, I guess. But obviously, I was too late. After your friend abandoned her at that motel, Em called me a couple of hours later and asked me to come get her and give her a lift home. She was pretty upset, and I think that woman took advantage of Em while she was drunk and raped her."

"Audie wouldn't do that," Reagan insisted, shaking her head. It took me over a month to get her in my own bed, she thought. "Did you tell the police any of this, or her parents?"

"I...uh...didn't want to get involved in that mess. I didn't know she would swallow a bunch of pills either," Tracey hedged.

"Em wouldn't have done that!"

"She talked about it all the time. Why are we rehashing all of this?" Tracey asked, clearly frustrated. "Emily's dead, and there's nothing we can do about it now." Tracey stepped closer to Reagan and wrapped her arms around her, rubbing her back. She slipped her hand under Reagan's hair, pulled it aside, and kissed the side of her neck tenderly. "I love you, Reagan," she mumbled. "I've always loved you. I want you so damn much. Now that Emily's gone and your new girlfriend has broken up with you, we can finally be together, the way we should have always been."

Reagan forced her hands up between them and pushed Tracey away. "I already told you I wasn't interested in you that way, Tracey, so back off! Now!"

Tracey released Reagan and stepped back, but Reagan could see the anger in her eyes. Reagan started to say something to take the sting out of what she'd already said, but before she could, Tracey slapped her with enough force to knock her off her feet. There were tears in her eyes and the taste of blood in her mouth. She started to get up, but Tracey dropped to her knees and straddled Reagan's hips.

"Get off me!" Reagan demanded hoarsely.

The look in Tracey's eyes was wild as she grabbed Reagan's blouse and ripped it open, sending buttons flying around the living room. "I've been waiting for this moment since I was eleven-fucking-years-old. If you won't give it up, I'll just take it." Tracey seethed as she slapped Reagan's hands away and roughly shoved her bra up to reveal her breasts.

When Reagan continued to fight her, Tracey balled up her fist and struck Reagan hard on the jaw and cheekbone, stunning her. Then she wrapped her hands around Reagan's throat, squeezing until breathing became too difficult and the darkness sucked her in.

****

Reagan had no idea what time it was. She coughed and fought to draw in a full breath. She turned her head slowly from side-to-side but didn't see or hear anyone in the house with her. She managed to bring a shaking hand up to her tender throat. It was hard to swallow, but she'd kill for a drink of water. She ached everywhere, and after several excruciating attempts, she forced her body over onto her stomach. She stopped moving to catch her breath.

She blinked rapidly to clear her vision enough to locate her cell phone. It lay against the baseboard. She shoved through the pain shooting through her body as she slowly inched her way toward the phone until it was within an arm's length of her body. She bit her bottom lip as she stretched as far as she could until the tips of her fingers touched the phone's case. However, with each attempt to reach the phone it slipped slightly farther away from her grasp.

Exhausted, Reagan rested her head on her outstretched arm to gather herself. She needed help. After a few minutes, she drew in as deep a breath as possible before making another stab at grabbing her elusive cell phone. Her mind rejoiced when her fingers finally grasped the phone case. She felt dizzy and lightheaded as she blinked again to clear her blurry vision. She forced her trembling index finger to press the name on her contact list. She exhaled with relief as she heard the number ring.

Answer, please answer, she thought as the number rang a second time. But before anyone answered, Reagan's mind suddenly went blank from exertion. Unable to think, she closed her eyes, letting the hand holding her phone drop to the floor beside her.

****

"Hey, baby," Audie said when she answered her phone. She smiled as she rubbed her cheek with the back of her hand and stared at the now half painted living room wall, welcoming the break. "Hello?" she asked a second time. The call hadn't disconnected, but there was no sound from Reagan. "Please say something, honey. I need to hear your voice." Still nothing. Audie disconnected the call, not in the mood to play games.

But somehow, she couldn't shake the idea that something was wrong. Reagan wasn't the type of woman to play stupid games, like calling and not speaking. She redialed Reagan's number, but all she heard was a busy signal and a message telling her to leave a message. Even if it was an accidental butt dial, Audie had to know. She stuffed her wallet into the back pocket of her paint smeared jeans and grabbed her car keys. "Let's go, Buck," she called, still afraid to leave the animal home alone. "Let's go check on a friend."

The drive from her house to Reagan's took about twenty minutes. Audie pulled her rental into the drive, parked behind Reagan's Beetle, and clipped a leash to Buck's collar. She paused at the front door, hesitant to knock. Buck danced around her feet and whined as he sniffed along the bottom of the closed door.

"Suck it up, Audie," she muttered to herself and knocked. When no one answered, she leaned down and cupped a hand on a window to peer inside. It wasn't until she glanced through the third front window that she saw the sofa was out of its usual place. She squatted for a better view and thought she saw a bare foot on the floor, jutting out behind an old armchair.

For a moment her heart stopped. She opened the storm door and checked the front doorknob. It was locked; somewhere deep inside Audie began to panic. She held Buck back and ordered him to sit. Then she took a step back and pushed against the wooden door. It gave a little under her weight but didn't open. As a last resort, she stepped back again and brought her foot up, slamming it against the door frame twice. On the second strike, the door popped open, and Audie rushed inside, finding a naked and battered Reagan lying behind the armchair.

Buck entered the house close behind Audie, quickly sniffing Reagan's body and licking her face. Even though she knew she probably shouldn't, Audie grabbed a small quilt from the back of the sofa and draped it over Reagan. She picked up Reagan's cell and dialed 9-1-1.

She locked Buck in her vehicle and sat on the floor with Reagan's head in her lap. Audie blinked away tears as she stroked Reagan's hair and whispered calming messages, assuring her she'd be all right, until the police and paramedics arrived. As she held Reagan, the young woman's eyes suddenly popped open, and she looked around wildly, blinking and clearly not recognizing Audie.

It wasn't until Audie moved away to allow the paramedics to treat Reagan that she finally took in the extent of Reagan's injuries. There were bruises and bite marks on her breasts, her abdomen, and the insides of her thighs. Bruises around her neck looked like fingerprints, as if someone attempted to strangle her. Dried blood was caked around her mouth and nose, and her left eye was swollen shut. Audie felt her stomach roil at the idea of what happened to Reagan, and she swallowed repeatedly to stop herself from vomiting.

Audie was forced to leave Reagan's side to answer questions from the police officers at the scene but kept an eye on what the paramedics were doing.

"Can you give us your name, ma'am?" an officer asked.

"Audra Wade," she answered.

"And what's your relationship with the victim?"

"I'm her significant other, I guess."

"Her girlfriend?"

"Yes."

"Can you give us her name?"

"Reagan Malloy, M-A-L-L-O-Y."

"You look very familiar to me," the officer said.

"My vehicle was vandalized here a few weeks ago. You may have responded to that."

"Yeah, yeah. I remember that now. Nice car. Do you have any idea who might have assaulted Ms. Malloy?"

"No. Reagan called me earlier today but didn't say anything. I was concerned and drove over to check on her. As far as I know, she didn't have any enemies."

The paramedics placed Reagan on a gurney and pushed it toward the door.

"Do you have any further questions? I'll be with her at the hospital," Audie said as she took Reagan's hand and held it until she was loaded into the ambulance.

She followed them to the nearest trauma center and called Suzanne. When Suzanne picked up her phone, she said, "Well, did you straighten out your little spat with Reagan?"

"Not exactly. Someone assaulted her this afternoon. I'm following the ambulance right now. Looks like we're going to Presbyterian Hospital. I'll try to let you know more later, but I really need a favor."

"What kind of favor?" Suzanne asked.

"I've got Buck with me. Would you please come pick him up and take him to your place until I can come get him? I'll take him for a walk before I leave him, and I'll leave the vehicle unlocked for you."

"He'll be fine. Call me later to let me know how Reagan is. I'm sure she's scared and will feel better knowing you're there for her."

After she parked, she let Buck have a quick tour around a grassy area. She returned him to her car and rushed into the emergency entrance.

She registered as being with Reagan, then waited for the clerk to see if there was any new information.

While she waited Audie used Reagan's cell phone to contact Reagan's brother, Ian. He arrived at the hospital within minutes. They waited together until an ER doctor finally came out to tell them how Reagan was doing.

Once they were gathered in the waiting room, the doctor said, "Miss Malloy has a severely bruised and swollen trachea, rendering her unable to speak at the moment. In addition, she suffered a concussion. She should regain her ability to speak once the swelling and bruising subsides, in a week, maybe two, depending on how careful she is. We plan to keep her sedated to allow her brain to recover. That's the good news."

"What's the bad news?" Ian asked.

"In my opinion, she was also sexually assaulted by her assailant. A rape kit has been run to document the numerous bruises and bite marks on her body. I will file my findings with the police, but they won't be able to get her story for several days. She may need to see a counselor to cope with her rape, but we'll know more later."

Audie listened calmly, but the idea of someone, anyone, doing that to Reagan enraged her. Reagan must have been terrified, and the thought of that was unacceptable.

****

It was almost dark by the time Reagan was admitted to a private room. Ian elected to return home to call his parents and touch base with several of his sister's friends to let them know she was hospitalized and unable to communicate. She was sedated to allow her time to rest and allow her injuries to begin to heal.

An oxygen cannula aided her breathing, while medication worked to reduce the swelling to her throat. Everything would heal in due time.

Although there wasn't much Audie could do for Reagan, she refused to leave her side, except to grab a quick, periodic snack. She didn't care that she was still wearing her painting clothes. She pulled a chair close to Reagan's bed, held her hand, her thumb tracing circles over Reagan's soft skin. Audie spent most of her time watching Reagan sleep.

Audie was dozing when the doctor came into Reagan's room on the second day of her stay.

"How's she doing?" Audie asked, clearing her throat.

"Are you a family member?" the doctor asked.

"She's my girlfriend," Audie answered.

"Close enough," the doctor said and sighed. "Her vital signs are doing better, and I'm going to reduce her sedation today. Hopefully her brain has stabilized enough that she'll wake up. However, we're never sure about damage caused by concussions. We'll keep an eye out for headaches, nausea, vomiting, or possible seizure activity. It's a little like her head is a snow globe that's been seriously shaken. Now it's trying to right itself, and all that fake snow is looking for its normal place to settle. Until that happens, she may be confused or agitated while she tries to make sense of what happened to her. It's even possible she won't remember anything about what caused her injuries. Our bodies can be very creative in deciding how to protect us.

"After we wean her off the sedatives, I believe placing her on steroids will help the swelling in her throat. Other than that, there isn't much we can do except give her body time to heal itself. Is her family planning to visit her?"

"Her brother lives in Round Rock and usually drops by after he leaves work. Her parents live in Houston, and I don't know if they're planning to drive up. I'll ask when Ian comes by this evening. If you think of anything else we should watch out for, let me know. I plan to stay here until she's released."

****

On the third day, Reagan's medication was lowered, in the hopes she would awaken. "The swelling has gone down significantly," the doctor said, smiling at Audie.

"Will she be able to speak?" Audie asked hopefully.

"It'll take a few weeks for her to be able to speak normally. I'd recommend she write things down as much as possible. It'll be difficult, but it's best she lets her vocal cords rest." He handed Audie a pen and pad of paper. "Be patient. She should wake up any time now. If you need anything, hit the nurse's call button."

Audie put the pen and paper aside, shook his hand, and returned her attention to Reagan.

That night, Audie moved her chair closer to Reagan's bed

and held her hand. She rested her chin on the rail to watch
Reagan sleep. "I love you, baby," Audie whispered. "I'm so
sorry I yelled at you, but I let my emotions get away from me.
If I'd kept them under control, this never would have happened
to you."

Audie eventually drifted off but was awakened by the
sound of a breathy, raspy voice saying "Aaw-dee."

She tried to release Reagan's hand, but the warm hand in
hers squeezed it with surprising strength. Audie sat up and
rubbed her face to fully wake up. "Oh, my God, baby! You're
awake! I want to hold you so much, but I don't want to hurt
you."

Reagan raised her other hand and tapped a finger against
her lips as she managed a slight smile.

Audie leaned over the rail to carefully kiss Reagan. "I love
you, baby," she whispered softly against Reagan's ear. When
she looked at her face, there were tears shimmering in
Reagan's eyes. "I'll get a nurse, okay?" Audie tried to remove
her hand from Reagan's grasp again, but Reagan held on and
shook her head.

"Stay," she managed to croak out.

"Don't try to talk now, sweetie," Audie said softly. "Let
your throat heal. Then we'll have all the time in the world to
talk as much as you want."

Reagan raised a hand and moved it around as if writing in
the air.

"You'll have to let my hand go so I can hand you a pen and
something to write on," Audie said. Seeing the panicked look
in Reagan's eyes, she added, "Just for a second. I promise."

Audie located the small pad of paper and pen on the
bedside table. She gave both to Reagan, who held the pad with
shaking hands and wrote: *Tracey...* Before she could write
anything else, Audie said, "She'll probably drop by to see you
soon. Your brother said he would contact your parents and
friends."

Reagan shook her head furiously and wrote:
Tracey...raped me.

Audie closed her eyes and ground her teeth together to
control her fury. She had to admit she'd never cared much for
Tracey. She saw the way she'd look at Reagan and touch her.

She was astounded at the accusation about the woman Reagan considered her best friend. Someone she trusted.

"She sexually assaulted you after she tried to kill you, Reagan," Audie said as calmly as she could manage.

I'm sorry, Reagan wrote with tears falling down her cheeks.

"*You* didn't do anything wrong, Reagan," Audie ground out through gritted teeth. "This wasn't your fault."

Don't leave, Reagan wrote, her eyes drooping closed. *So tired.* She laid the pad on her chest and found Audie's hand again.

"I'm right here, honey."

"Love you," Reagan mouthed before turning her head slightly and closing her eyes, clinging to Audie's hand.

"I love you too, baby," Audie whispered as she placed a soft kiss on Reagan's lips.

****

Audie was jolted awake bright and early the following morning when the police arrived at the hospital to question Reagan. She wrote the answers to their questions as completely as she could. She named Tracey Chaisson as her attacker and gave the gist of the argument that led to her attack. She couldn't remember anything after being choked but agreed to provide an oral statement once the doctors cleared her to speak again.

When the police left her room, Reagan cried and reached out for Audie. Audie gently pulled Reagan into her arms and offered comforting words to her.

"I think you might feel better if you took a nice, warm shower and cleaned up a little. Would you like that, sweetie?" Audie asked with a smile. "I can help, if you want."

Reagan nodded, and Audie followed her to the shower in her hospital bathroom. Reagan blushed when she removed her hospital gown and revealed her injured body. Seeing Reagan's bruises and cuts infuriated Audie, but she said, "You're so beautiful, baby," which brought a tremulous smile to Reagan's lips.

After Reagan stepped out of the shower, Audie dried her

thoroughly with a towel and had her sit on the toilet seat to comb and brush her hair. Audie led her back into her hospital room and carefully rubbed lotion onto her skin. Then Audie drew Reagan onto her lap and held her in her arms until she fell peacefully asleep again. Not long afterward, Audie closed her eyes and whispered, "I love you."

****

After four days in the hospital, Reagan was discharged with strong orders to not use her voice unnecessarily. Audie helped Reagan into her car and drove her home. They weren't far from the hospital when Audie decided she didn't want Reagan to be alone.

"I don't think you should be by yourself for a while. Would you like to go back to the coast for a couple of weeks? I can take care of both you and Buck. I'm a decent cook, so you won't starve, and I can work from the house while you rest," Audie said as she held Reagan's hand. "You'll just need to pack enough clothes. Then I'll pack and load Buck."

Reagan squeezed Audie's hand and nodded. "Can...I...sleep...with you?" Reagan managed.

"If you want to." Audie smiled.

Reagan nodded and smiled back before resting her head against Audie's shoulder.

Ninety minutes later, they were heading south toward San Antonio.

****

Audie smiled as she glanced down at Reagan who slept peacefully beside her with her left hand resting on Audie's thigh. Audie couldn't remember the last time she'd felt so content. She didn't want to lose that feeling again.

Audie hated waking Reagan after she brought her vehicle to a stop next to the bungalow's deck. She ran her fingers through Reagan's hair until she responded and blinked her eyes open.

"Is falling asleep every time we drive down here going to become a habit?" Audie asked with a smile. "I might develop a complex or something."

"Not...you," Reagan answered as she sat up and cleared her throat. "Peaceful...here."

"Don't talk. I was just kidding." Audie chuckled lightly. "Besides, I enjoy watching you sleep."

Audie stepped out of the car and opened the back door to release Buck. He leapt out and raised his snout to sniff the Gulf air before he was off to explore. "I'll carry in our bags," she said to Reagan. "Take your time."

Reagan nodded and opened the front passenger door. She brought a hand up to shade her eyes from the sun, then strolled down toward the Gulf, followed by Buck. She was rubbing her hands up and down her bare arms when Audie embraced her from behind. Reagan leaned back against Audie, tilting her head to look up at her. "Chilly," she said breathily.

"Come inside and I'll get a fire going," Audie said.

"Hot...chocolate?"

"Of course," Audie said, leaning down to kiss Reagan lightly. "It should feel good on your throat."

Audie whistled for Buck and pulled Reagan closer against her side to keep her warm until they reached the bungalow. After starting a low fire in the fireplace, Audie made two cups of hot chocolate and settled beside Reagan on the sofa. By the time they finished their hot chocolate, Reagan had snuggled up against Audie's side again. "Love you," she whispered, looking up at Audie.

"I didn't think I'd ever say this again to anyone, but I love you, too, baby," Audie said softly.

Reagan raised up on her knees. "Kiss...me."

"Is that really such a good idea?" Audie asked.

"Just...kiss...me."

Audie kissed her lightly. Reagan jerked away and slapped her on the chest. "Kiss me...like you...mean it, dammit," she demanded hoarsely.

"I don't want to get carried away and hurt you," Audie said and rubbed her chest, which still stung.

"Touch...me. I...need...you," Reagan implored.

Audie ran one hand to the back of Reagan's neck and slipped the other hand under her blouse, breathing hard as she drew Reagan onto her lap. She teased Reagan's lips with the tip of her tongue and teeth without taking her mouth fully with her own. Her hand slid up Reagan's side until her fingers found the soft pliant skin of her breast. She pulled back slightly and stared at Reagan.

"Don't...stop," Reagan encouraged after Audie discovered Reagan wasn't wearing a bra.

Audie grinned as she finally gave up and began a slow, deliberate exploration of Reagan's mouth while she filled the palm of her hand with the warmth of Reagan's full breast. Reagan buried her hands in Audie's hair and held her in place as she deepened their kiss. When they finally broke apart, Audie gasped and then said, "I want you so much, baby. I'm sorry I drove you away. Please forgive me."

"Bed," Reagan said, standing to take Audie's hand and pulling her up. She wrapped her arms around Audie's waist and kissed her again, deeply as she backed them toward the bedroom. Before Audie could do anything, Reagan unzipped her jeans, slowly pushing them down, and shoved Audie down on the bed. Reagan ran her hands up Audie's thighs then dropped to her knees between Audie's legs. Audie's protest died on her lips when Reagan's mouth attached to its target and sucked her into her mouth.

Then she stopped and withdrew her mouth. She sat back on her legs and stared at Audie with tears in her eyes. "I'm...sorry. I...can't." Tears flowed down her cheeks. "Not...right. Be...patient...with...me." Audie pulled Reagan up and kissed her tenderly while softly stroking her cheeks.

She wanted Reagan and knew Reagan wanted her, but the time wasn't right. Audie knew that Reagan was still fighting the memory of her trauma.

Reagan laid her head on Audie's shoulder. "I...forgive...you," she said and sniffed as Audie cradled her in her arms.

****

Reagan was awakened well after dark by a hand lazily drifting up and down her side, followed by warm lips encircling her nipple. She brought her hand up to press Audie's lips harder against her breast. "More," she said and sighed, opening her eyes to see her lover's face in the faint moonlight shining through the bedroom window. She blinked in horror when she saw Tracey's angry face hovering over her, felt her hands moving to her throat, and squeezing.

"No," Reagan screamed as her body quickly lurched up, shaking and gasping for breath while clawing wild-eyed at her throat.

"What's wrong, baby?" Audie asked, sitting up and rubbing a hand through her hair to wake up, reaching out to wrap her arms around Reagan to comfort her.

Reagan slapped her arms away and hissed, "Don't...touch...me," before getting out of bed. She made her way into the adjoining bathroom to splash cold water on her face.

"Are you all right, honey?" Audie asked from behind her.

"Bad...dream," Reagan admitted. "Sorry."

"Want to talk about it?" Audie asked softly. "You might feel better if you do."

Reagan shook her head, splashing more cold water on her face in an attempt to wash away the image of Tracey looming over her. Patting her face dry, Reagan looked up at Audie, her eyes unfocused. "Need...sleep."

"Okay. We can talk tomorrow," Audie said as she moved away to let Reagan exit the bathroom.

Reagan climbed back into bed and pulled the sheet and blanket up tightly under her chin, turning onto her side and facing away from Audie.

In the middle of the night, Reagan rolled over closer to Audie and rested her head on Audie's shoulder. Her hand worked its way up Audie's abdomen, stopping when her fingers reached the base of her collarbones.

"I'm...sorry," Reagan whispered softly, the movement of her lips grazing the skin of Audie's neck, creating an unexpected shiver. "Please...talk...to me."

"I love you," Audie said. "You don't have anything to be sorry for."

"I...overreacted. It was...a stupid...dream," Reagan tried to explain as she raised her head, resting it in the palm of her hand.

"It was just your mind trying to come to grips

with…something horrible," Audie said, her finger moving Reagan's hair back from her face. "I don't know how to help you."

Reagan's mouth opened and closed soundlessly as she struggled to speak. Suddenly her voice erupted harshly. "S…She…*raped*…me!" Tears filled her eyes again. She raised a hand and covered her eyes. "Why…didn't…I…see that…in her eyes? Was it…my fault?"

"No. She was your friend, and you trusted her. You couldn't have known what was in her mind, honey, so don't ever blame yourself," Audie said softly as her fingers stroked Reagan's arm.

"I don't…deserve you…Audie. Now you're…stuck with…me…a b-broken…woman," Reagan said through tears.

Audie pulled Reagan into her arms and kissed the top of her head. "I chose you, Reagan, and even though I almost lost you because I allowed my memories to come between us, I still love you. Try to go to sleep and rest your voice."

****

The smell of fresh coffee and tempting bacon roused Reagan from a peaceful sleep. The bright sun against a deep blue sky, accompanied by the periodic squawking of seagulls, brought a slow, easy smile to Reagan's lips. She stretched, preparing to get up and dress when Audie appeared in the bedroom door, fully clothed and holding a tray of food.

"Looks like you might be ready for a little breakfast," Audie said cheerfully. "Mind if I join you?"

Reagan patted the bed and said, "Please."

Audie set the lap tray across Reagan's body, then picked up her cup of coffee, folded a leg under her, and sat at the foot of the bed. "Feeling better?" Audie asked and sipped her coffee.

"Much," Reagan said, nibbling a piece of bacon. "Sorry about…last night," she added.

Audie smiled. "I love you, Reagan. Tell me what happened."

"Nightmare," Reagan replied, swallowing hard. "Tracey…choking me. I couldn't…get away. So…afraid."

"Your doctor told me you might have a delayed reaction of some kind. When we get back to Austin, you should speak to the counselor he suggested," Audie said calmly before setting her coffee mug down and reaching out to touch Reagan's arm. "It wasn't your fault, baby," she said softly.

"She had...a picture of you...with Emily...going into a...motel room. Did you...sleep...with Emily?" Reagan asked with a trembling voice.

Audie lowered her head for a moment before answering. "I don't know," she finally answered.

"No lies," Reagan said and sniffed.

"I honest-to-God do not know, but I may have," Audie said, inhaling a deep breath. "A few months before Carlie died, I was feeling so helpless and overwhelmed by her illness, work, and life in general. I went out one evening and got drunk. I vaguely remember picking someone up. She may have told me her name, but I didn't care enough to remember it. All I wanted, or needed, was just one night of anonymous sex—with anyone—to relieve my unbearable stress and loneliness. I swear to God she was asleep and uninjured when I left. I didn't hurt her. I was ashamed of what I did, but I couldn't undo it. I left her with enough money to get home after she woke up, but that wasn't enough because I'm sure I used her. I thought she'd be okay, and, truthfully, as cold as it sounds, I've never really thought about that night again."

"Thank...you...for telling me. I know...you didn't...hurt Emily," Reagan said between sips of warm coffee. "Tracey...did...because of...me."

Cupping Reagan's cheek in her hand, Audie said, "It wasn't your fault, honey. Okay?"

Reagan looked at Audie and brought her hand up to cover Audie's for a moment.

"Feel strong enough for a short walk on the beach?" Audie asked as she stood and picked up the tray from Reagan's lap.

Reagan held up her thumb and forefinger an inch apart with a nod.

"Get dressed while I clean up the kitchen. It's still a little brisk out, so you might consider your sweats and a light jacket," Audie said before leaving the room.

****

Half an hour later, Audie opened the deck doors and escorted Reagan outside. Buck trotted easily in front of them, searching for unwary gulls. Reagan clasped Audie's hand, holding it until they were strolling along the edge of the water. The breeze blowing in off the Gulf was cool, but clean smelling. Audie was mildly surprised when Reagan released her hand then wrapped an arm around her waist, snuggling closer. Audie cautiously draped her arm over Reagan's shoulder, gazing out at the Gulf, feeling the scattered pieces of her life beginning to fall into place. She gently ran her hand over Reagan's shoulder.

Reagan stopped walking. Audie faced her and raised an eyebrow in question. Reagan finally smiled and stepped closer to Audie, placing both palms on Audie's chest. "I...love...you, Audie. You are...the one...I've waited for...the love...of my life," Reagan slowly managed. "My...Carlie."

Audie felt her eyes burn as they involuntarily began to tear up. She sucked in a deep, calming breath before speaking. "I hope I can be," she said. "It's an honor I won't take lightly."

Reagan ran her hands under Audie's jacket as Audie leaned down and kissed her tenderly.

****

The following day, Audie entered the bungalow after a quick trip to town. "I thought we might try something a little different today," she said with a smile on her face.

"What?" Reagan asked.

"Come outside and I'll show you. It *was* your idea." Audie covered Reagan's eyes with her hands and walked her onto the deck. When she dropped her hands, there were two brand-new, shiny bicycles parked at the base of the deck steps. "Since jogging isn't your thing, and since, as you informed me, we live in the bicycle capital of Texas, I decided we could use them. Pick the one you like, and I'll adjust it for your height. There's a pretty nice bicycle trail just up from the coastline."

They attached water bottles to the bikes, snapped helmets

on, and were ready to roll. It had been years since Audie rode a bicycle, and Reagan laughed while Audie struggled to pedal in a relatively straight line. Reagan rode large circles around a frustrated Audie.

"Whoever said something was as easy as riding a bicycle must have been crazy," Audie said and laughed. "More like easy as falling *off* a bicycle."

"You must have ridden one...when you were little," Reagan teased.

"Yeah, when I was about six-years-old and maybe four feet tall. Go ahead. I'll catch up with you in a few minutes...maybe."

Audie eventually found her confidence after two falls and one scrapped knee. She pedaled as fast as she could until she came upon Reagan lounging on a bench alongside the bike trail, her head thrown back to soak up the sunshine. She looked at Audie with a smile. "Glad you made it...before I...fell asleep."

"Hey, your voice is sounding better," Audie noted.

"I know. Must be the fresh sea air." Reagan grinned. "Glad we came."

"Let's take a leisurely ride before I forget how again." Audie motioned with her arm. "Lead the way."

Reagan jumped on her bike and took off. Amazingly, Audie caught up to her quickly but stayed back a little. She discovered she enjoyed watching the movements of Reagan's ass. In fact, Audie found the movement of Reagan's ass muscles extremely alluring and grew slightly uncomfortable after realizing how much the sight aroused her.

A mile or two from the bungalow they stopped to gaze out over the Gulf. Reagan snuggled close and ran a hand under Audie's T-shirt to tease her nipples while her other hand dropped to cup her crotch.

"What are you doing?" Audie asked, trying to back away from Reagan's wandering hands.

"No one's...here. I thought...I might...molest...you a little," Reagan said. "I could feel you...staring at my ass...while we were riding. Isn't this...what you were... thinking about?"

"Perhaps someplace a little more private, but not out here

in front of God and everyone though," Audie protested. "You know I want you, but I don't want to do anything that might hurt you. I'm willing to wait until I know you're ready."

"You're killin' me, baby," Reagan said in frustration. "If you really love me…as much as you claim you do…then I need you to act like it. I need to feel your body…on mine. I promise I won't break."

"If I really love you? Don't ever doubt how much I love you, but what you went through affected both of us. You know how aggressive I can get. I don't want to do anything that might freak you out unexpectedly. When I make love to you again, I want to know you're right there with me, completely. I never want you to be afraid of me, baby. Can you understand that?"

****

That night, Audie stretched out on the bed. When Reagan rolled over to settle comfortably in her arms and began stroking her nails down Audie's body, inviting her to become more intimate, she felt Audie's muscles begin to twitch and smiled knowing her lover wouldn't be able to resist much longer.

Audie finally moved closer, covering Reagan's body with her own and kissing her neck as her fingers slid up to Reagan's throat. Reagan's body stiffened, and she rolled off her.

Audie turned on her side and looked at Reagan. "When you give yourself to me, I don't want you to be afraid of what might happen. Love without trust can't survive, baby."

"Do you expect me to just forget what happened?" Reagan snapped.

"I know you'll never forget it, but I hope you'll find a way to trust again. A way to trust that *I* will never hurt you because I love you."

****

Reagan rolled onto her back and stretched her body to its full length to awaken. She smiled when she heard the French doors to the bungalow snap closed quietly. "It's all right, baby.

I'm awake," she said. When there was no response from Audie, she threw the covers back and swung her legs off the bed, pausing to rub her hands over her face before standing. She reached down to pick up the T-shirt she'd worn the day before off the floor and pulled it over her head before stepping into her sweatpants. "Audie?" she said, tying the waist of her sweats.

"Mornin', baby," a familiar voice that raised the hair on the back of her neck said.

Reagan looked up to face the intruder. "What the hell are you doing here, Tracey?"

"I came to take you home, where you belong," Tracey said.

Reagan's eyes flicked down to the gun in Tracey's hand. "Then you came a long way for nothing. I'm not going anywhere with you."

"I think you will after I get rid of your friend...permanently." Tracey smiled, jabbing her weapon around erratically.

"You're crazy," Reagan said coldly. "You killed Emily, and she never did anything to you."

"That was your fault. You chose that simpering, pathetic weakling over me," Tracey said, her voice raised. "She fucked other women behind your back every damn chance she got, including the one you're shacking up with now."

"Emily was my *friend*. I wasn't in love with her, but she didn't deserve to die."

"I'm your friend, too, Reagan."

Reagan closed her eyes and took a deep breath, but the hurt and anger she'd been fighting overcame her, and she couldn't contain it any longer. She took a step closer to Tracey and forced the hateful words out. "You *raped* me," she seethed tightly, bringing her hands up to shove Tracey away from her, ignoring her weapon.

"You forced me to do that! I had to show you."

"Show me what? That you could hurt me!" Reagan said, shoving Tracey again.

"Stop it, Reagan," Tracey said, knocking Reagan's hands away.

"You almost killed me, you stupid bitch. I don't love you. I'll never love you. What part of that don't you understand?"

Reagan shook her head. "I'm in love with Audie. Totally and passionately. You may have taken me against my will, but it sure as shit wasn't love. You're the only pathetic weakling in my life!"

Tracey swung her hand holding the gun at Reagan, slicing through her cheek and knocking her to the floor of the living room. Reagan touched her cheek and felt the blood there. She tried to push herself up, but Tracey kicked her back down and stood over Reagan, breathing heavily as she aimed the gun at her.

"I loved you," Tracey croaked.

"But Reagan doesn't want you," Audie growled, standing just inside the French doors behind Tracey.

Tracey spun around and brought her weapon up to aim it at Audie's chest.

"Buck! Protect!" Audie ordered.

Buck raced into the bungalow and clamped his teeth into Tracey's leg, snarling as he shook his head. Reagan scrambled to her feet and grabbed the fireplace poker and swung it with all her might, striking Tracey across the back.

Audie lunged forward and grabbed Tracey's wrist and twisted it hard, forcing her to drop her handgun. Audie backhanded Tracey, knocking her down.

Tracey felt around for her weapon, and in that moment, Audie exploded, releasing her fury. She grabbed Tracey by the front of her shirt and slammed a fist into her face, again and again. "You vandalized my car, shot my dog, destroyed a precious gift from my wife. But worst of all you violated and tried to kill Reagan," Audie ground out, breathing heavily, until Tracey's face was battered and bloodied.

Reagan stopped Audie from striking the obviously unconscious woman again by wrapping her arms around Audie's shaking body. Audie's knuckles were cut and bruised, but the feel of Reagan against her calmed her.

Audie removed her button-down shirt and pressed it against Reagan's cheek to stop the bleeding. "We need to call the police," Audie mumbled, returning Reagan's embrace. "I love you. Let's finally put an end to this nightmare."

Reagan grabbed her cell phone off the dresser and sat beside Audie, who pulled Buck close. Reagan leaned against her as she made the call.

"I'm never letting you go, Reagan. You're giving me a second chance, and I'm going to embrace it." Tears streamed down Audie's cheeks. "I almost lost everything because of one stupid mistake, and I won't ever let that happen again. I love you."

"I love you too, baby."

Epilogue

Four months later

"Ready, honey?" Audie asked as she entered the kitchen of her home in Austin. She stopped behind Reagan and pushed her hair aside to kiss the side of her neck.

"Almost. Are they here already?" Reagan asked, raising a hand to cup Audie's cheek in her palm. "What if they don't like me?" she added with concern in her voice.

"Trust me, they'll love you as much as I do," Audie said as she pulled Reagan against her.

Reagan turned around in Audie's arms and kissed her tenderly. "Happy birthday, baby," she whispered in Audie's ear as she hugged her, loving how safe she now felt. "But you'll have to wait until later for your present from me, so we won't be interrupted." She grinned slyly.

Their moment alone was interrupted by the front door bell chiming. "Let the games begin," Audie said, taking a deep breath. She wrapped an arm around Reagan's waist and walked through the open dining room to the front door. Audie opened it, stepping outside to briefly hug Amanda and Christina Lange, who were lugging a large cooler between them.

"There's another cooler in the back seat of the Bronco." Amanda smiled as she hugged Audie.

"I'll get it," Audie volunteered. Looking at Reagan as she walked backwards to the car, she said, "Show them where to put the shrimp, honey."

Reagan stepped forward and hugged both women before leading them through the house toward the kitchen. "We have a huge metal container filled with ice outside where we can dump these later after everyone else arrives. Just set the cooler beside the fridge for now."

By the time Amanda and her sister set the cooler down, Audie walked in with Suzanne, carrying the second cooler, followed by Gia, who was carrying a bottle of wine in each hand. Gia paused in the foyer and looked around. When she entered the kitchen she said, "What did you do to the living room, Audra? The lighting is brighter."

"Do you like it?" Audie asked as Suzanne and Gia hugged Reagan warmly.

"It is very warm and inviting." Gia nodded.

"Then you can thank Reagan. She designed the new panels to reflect the coast," Audie said and smiled. "I love the openness they bring to the room."

"I thought you were getting the old ones redone," Suzanne said.

"I did. They're hanging in my office and the guest bedroom."

Audie cleared her throat. "Now for why you're here for this family celebration. Suzanne, Gia, let me introduce you to Carlie's daughter, Amanda Lange, and her sister, Christina. Amanda, Chris, this is my business partner and friend, Suzanne Travers, and her wife, Gianna."

As the women became acquainted, the door chime sounded again. Reagan placed her hand on Audie's back and said, "I'll get it, baby."

Reagan walked quickly back to the front door and swung it open, smiling brightly as she extended her hand to a middle-aged couple and announced, "Welcome. I'm Reagan Malloy, Audie's friend."

The woman pushed Reagan's hand away and enclosed Reagan in a warm embrace. "You're as beautiful as Audie said you were. I'm Lynn Peterson, Audie's sister-in-law, and this is Jerry, my husband. We're so glad that Audie found someone who could make her smile again."

"Thank you, Lynn. I'm honored to finally meet you both," Reagan responded with a genuine smile. Before they could enter Audie's house, another car pulled into the semi-circular drive in front of the house.

"Those are my folks," Lynn said. "And, if I know my mom, she brought a few things to contribute to the feast."

"I assume you know your way around the house, so go on in while I help your parents," Reagan said cheerfully, stepping around Lynn and Jerry.

"I'm Audie's…um…girlfriend, Reagan Malloy. Can I help you carry anything inside?" she asked, meeting the older couple at the rear cargo door of their Suburban.

"That's very sweet of you, dear. Thank you," Betty said, handing two large trays to Reagan.

"I love deviled eggs," Reagan said when she saw the tray of eggs. "These look delicious."

"They're Audie's favorite, too," Betty said. "I'm sorry. I should have introduced myself before loading you down with stuff. I'm Betty Carlson, Audie's mother-in-law, and that's my husband, Don."

"A pleasure to finally meet you both," Reagan said and nodded.

"Don, are you getting the cake?" Betty asked. "I've got the ice cream and potato salad."

Don Carlson waved a hand over the roof of the car as he stood to close the rear passenger door and smiled at Reagan. Just as they started for the front door, Audie jogged down the walkway, stopping long enough to snatch a deviled egg from one of the trays Reagan was carrying and stuffing it into her mouth. "Fabulous, as always, Betty!"

"I guess you'll have to teach me how to make these, Mrs. Carlson," Reagan said over her shoulder.

"Any time, but please call me Betty, dear. We're all family here." Betty grinned, pausing to hug Audie tightly. "Is she here?" she asked.

"Out on the patio and as nervous as a cat at a dog fight," Audie said.

Reagan led the little line of people into the house and to the kitchen. Lynn met them, and she and Reagan began putting everything into the refrigerator or freezer. Audie popped open a Corona for Don and two others for herself and Reagan, while Lynn prepared a glass of tea for Betty.

Betty took a drink and a deep breath, held her husband's hand, and walked resolutely out the back door onto the large inlaid rock patio. When Amanda stood and turned to face them, Betty released Don's hand and set her drink down, then strode to her. Betty's arms suddenly enclosed Amanda's body and held her. Amanda looked a little shocked but brought her arms up to return the hug.

"She looks even more like Carlie in person," Don said, leaning over to Audie, who was grinning widely with an arm draped over Reagan's shoulder.

"Well, go on over and say hello to your granddaughter, Don," Audie said. "She's come a long way to meet you."

Don nodded before sauntering across the patio to embrace his wife and granddaughter. It wasn't long until their tears were replaced by joyous laughter.

"Too bad Carlie couldn't have seen this," Reagan said, looking up at Audie.

"I think she knew it would happen eventually. Thanks for helping me make it work, honey. I love you," Audie said before leaning down to kiss Reagan lightly. "I'm so happy you agreed to move in here with me, so we could begin building a new life...together."

"You have a wonderful, accepting family, sweetheart. Thank you for inviting me to be a part of it. Life with you will be an adventure, and I look forward to spending every minute of it with you," Reagan said, hugging Audie tightly. "I love you, too."

About the Author

Originally from the Appalachian region of Eastern Tennessee, Brenda and her wife, Cheryl, recently moved to Central Michigan to be closer to family. She began writing in junior high school where she wrote an admittedly hokey western serial to entertain her friends, Completing her graduate studies in Eastern European history in 1971, she worked as a graphic artist, a public relations specialist for the military and a display advertising specialist until she finally had to admit her mother might have been right and earned her teaching certification. She retired from teaching world history and political science in 2013 after thirty years. Brenda and Cheryl celebrated their twentieth anniversary by getting legally married in June of 2017. They are the parents of four grown children, Kenneth, Amy, Laura, and Jamie, and the grandparents of eight grandchildren. Rounding out their home is a ten-year-old laid-back cat named Tudie and a seven-year-old Puggle named Peanut, who snores like a freight train. Brenda may be contacted at adcockb10@yahoo.com and welcomes all comments.

Books by Brenda Adcock

One Step At A Time

Maddie James, a former rising rock star, saw her career crash and burn after a night of drug-induced recklessness. Now she has just been released after spending ten long years in prison and a lifetime of poor choices, her career and future gone. She takes her first steps to establish a new life, unable to trust anyone and remaining the sullen, impulsive woman she had always been. She is determined to forget her past and take control her life on her own terms again. When she is hired by a traveling carnival group, she's accepted despite her past and is finally befriended by people who don't judge her. But memories from the past haunt her and she leaves the carnival in the middle of the night, not realizing her past will always follow her.

Danielle Hunter is a part of Maddie's past, a teenager when they first met and now a woman in her mid-twenties, beginning a new and promising career. Dani discovers that Maddie has returned to the town where everything she wanted had been destroyed and despite her fascination with fallen rocker, Maddie pushes her away…until Maddie is arrested for the murder of a woman she had a dispute with while incarcerated. Now broken and defeated, Maddie gives up on a future of any kind. Can Dani do anything to save Maddie from returning to prison for a crime she didn't commit or let Maddie continue her destructive journey down the endless road of bad decisions?

Unresolved Conflicts

The long awaited sequel to *Redress of Grievances*

Thomas Wolfe said: "You can't go home again," and most of us know that, but it doesn't mean wanting to recapture just one good memory about our family isn't powerful enough to draw us back over and over again.

Harriett Markham and her lover, Jess Raines have finally settled into a comfortable relationship together following a harrowing and disturbing case when their peaceful life is interrupted by a plea from a high school friend of Harriett's, who has been arrested for the murder of a fellow teacher. Their investigation drags them both into a past they'd rather forget and forces them to acknowledge their seemingly perfect life might not be quite so perfect to the rest of their family.

Every family has secrets they'd prefer to not share, even with the people they love most. A trip to Harriett's home town re-opens old wounds for both Harriett and Jess that will either force their families together again or rip them apart forever.

Redress of Grievances

Harriett Markham is a defense attorney in Austin, Texas, who lost everything eleven years earlier. She had been an associate with a Dallas firm and involved in an affair with a senior partner, Alexis Dunne. Harriett represented a rape/murder client named Jared Wilkes and got the charges dismissed on a technicality. When Wilkes committed a rape and murder after his release, Harriett was devastated. She resigned and moved to Austin, leaving everything behind, including her lover.

Despite lingering feelings for Alexis, Harriett becomes involved with a sex-offense investigator, Jessie Raines, a woman struggling with secrets of her own. Harriett thinks she might finally be happy, but then Alexis re-enters her life. She refers a case of multiple homicide allegedly committed by Sharon Taggart, a woman with no motive for the crimes. Harriett is creeped out by the brutal murders, but reluctantly agrees to handle the defense.

As Harriett's team prepares for trial, disturbing information comes to light. Sharon denies any involvement in the crimes, but the evidence against her seems overwhelming. Harriett is plunged into a case rife with twisty psychological motives, questionable sanity, and a client with a complex and disturbing life. Is she guilty or not? And will Harriett's legal defense bring about justice—or another Wilkes case?

Recipient of a 2008 award from the Golden Crown Literary Society, the premiere organization for the support and nourishment of quality lesbian literature. *Redress of Grievances* won in the category of Lesbian Mystery.

Gift of the Redeemer

Jourdaine Troyce is the commandant of the Guardians, her entire life spent training to kill, literally, anyone that poses the slightest threat to her emperor or the royal family. Killing is as natural as breathing.

Ambreen Prins is a pacifist by nature, killing only as a last resort as she and her young companions fight against the tyranny of the emperor.

Rowan Shayne is the captain of an Intergalactic ship crewed by all the misfits the Fleet can't put anywhere else. They aren't expected to do great things. They're not even expected to function well enough to do their jobs.

Alec Travers is one of the best fighter pilots the Fleet has ever seen, especially when flanked by her two closest friends, creating what they call The Furies. But being posted to Captain Shayne's ship of misfits, out where there are no enemies to fight, is stifling. All she and the other Furies want is to get out there and take down the enemy. Whoever that enemy might be.

Heartbreak, treachery, evil, and the need for justice bring these four together on an adventure to discover the gift of the Redeemer, and the heroines they are destined to become.

The Heart of the Mountain

Lucinda "Lu" Calder is an experienced miner, sent to investigate possible irregularities at Brushy #3, a coal mine owned by her stepfather, in eastern Kentucky. Acting as a transfer from another mine in the West, she is hired as a general miner and mechanic. As the first, and only, female miner at Brushy #3, she puts up with some distrust and hazing from her male counterparts to test her mettle.

One of the first people she meets is an attractive woman in personnel named Regina Kinlaw. Regina is the single mother of a nine-year-old daughter, who is relentlessly curious. When Regina's van breaks down, Lu stops to assist and is drawn to the young woman. Even though Regina seems stand-offish and secretive, something about her intrigues Lu. But she has a job to do and can't allow herself to be distracted by wishful thinking.

The area surrounding Brushy #3 is a close knit, rural community and Lu finds herself thrown into situations that bring her into more frequent contact with Regina than she planned. They also bring her into contact with a man who believes Regina is his future wife and resents the time Regina spends with Lu. It's a situation that jeopardizes Lu's mission, and eventually her life.

Untouchable

Dr. Emma Rothenberg is the most feared professor at Overland University beause of her failure rate. Laramie "Ramie" Sunderlund is a senior art major, desperate to earn three lousy English credits to graduate. Thrown together in a battle of wills, the two women grudgingly establish a measure of respect for one another during one long semester.

Emma is a lonely woman of forty-five who occasionally risks her career with dangerous liaisons. Ramie faces unwanted advances from Rothenberg's graduate assistant, resulting in an assault that threatens her future as a sculptress.

Relieved when the semester ends and Ramie leaves to recuperate at home, Emma is suddenly faced with the fact that she misses the woman with curly blonde hair and deep blue eyes who occupied an aisle seat on the third row. She was also a young woman half her age, virtually a child. The notion of anything between them is ridiculous.

When Ramie returns to the university a decade later as the artist-in-residence, Emma is shocked that the younger woman seems interested in actively pursuing her. Against the objections of parents, friends, and colleagues, and despite their own reservations, what are these two very different women willing to sacrifice to find the happiness both are seeking?

In the Midnight Hour

What happens when you wake up to find the woman of your dreams in your bed? All-night radio hostess Desdemona, Queen of the Night draws her listening audience with her sultry, seductive voice, the only thing of value she possesses. During the day she becomes an insecure, unattractive woman named Marsha Barrett, living in a world with too many mirrors. She is comfortable with her obscurity until she meets Colleen Walters, a tall, attractive woman hired to expand her listening audience by selling Desdemona to new markets. When she wakes up in bed with Colleen after a night at a club, Marsha is terrified. A woman like Colleen would never go to bed with a woman like Marsha. She might dream about such a thing, but in the harsh reality of daylight, it would never happen. Beauty is only drawn to beauty and Marsha refuses to believe beauty could ever be drawn to anyone who looks like her. Just as she begins to believe happiness may be possible, the past returns determined to destroy them.

The Chameleon

Six years ago Detective Christine Shaw left her happy life and a good job in Texas to follow her libido to New York City. She's still a cop, but her stewardess girlfriend has flown the coop . and Chris hasn't been able to fill the void. Everything in her life begins to change when she and her partner are assigned to a high profile case.

The murder of Broadway star Elaine Barrie propels Chris into a whole new world. A fan of the murdered actress since she was a teenager, Chris isn't prepared for the secrets she uncovers during their investigation, including her attraction to the daughter of her number one suspect.

Was the victim any of the personalities witnesses describe, or was the real person a chameleon, satisfying the expectations of each person she met?

The Game of Denial

Joan Carmichael, a successful New York businesswoman, lost the love of her life ten years earlier. Alone, she raised their four children, always cherishing her deep love for her wife. Her memories of their life together come back even stronger as one of their daughters prepares to marry. Joan and her four adult kids fly to Virginia to meet the groom's family and attend the ceremony at the small horse farm owned by the mother of the fiancé.

Evelyn "Evey" Chase, also a widow, has secrets in her past, and her memories of her dead husband aren't pleasant. She's concerned about meeting her future daughter-in-law's family, certain that she and her three kids will have little in common with the wealthy New Yorkers.

Besides, the thought of two women in a relationship bringing up a family together makes her uncomfortable, even though her daughter-in-law assures her that lesbianism is not hereditary or catching. When the two women meet they are drawn to one another in a way neither anticipated, and the game of denial begins. Evey fights her attraction and doesn't realize the effect she has on Joan. Joan tries to shake off her feelings, seeing them as a betrayal to the memory of her wife. Besides, isn't Evey Chase straight? After Evey and Joan share an intimate moment at the wedding reception, they are both emotionally terrified and Joan flees. Will Joan overcome the feeling of betraying her former mate and stop denying her desire to be happy again? Can Evey finally face her past in order to accept the love of another woman and the desire to live the life she had once dreamed of?

The Sea Hawk

Dr. Julia Blanchard, a marine archaeologist, and her team of divers have spent almost eighteen months excavating the remains of a ship found a few miles off the coast of Georgia. Although they learn quite a bit about the nineteenth century sailing vessel, they have found nothing that would reveal the identity of the ship they have nicknamed "The Georgia Peach."

Her rescue at sea leads her on an unexpected journey into the true identity of the Peach and the captain and crew who called it their home. Her travels take her to the island of Martinique, the eastern Caribbean islands, the Louisiana German Coast and New Orleans at the close of the War of 1812.

How had the Peach come to rest in the waters off the Georgia coast? What had become of her alluring and enigmatic captain, Simone Moreau? Can love conquer everything, even time?

Pipeline

What do you do when the mistakes you made in the past come back to slap you in the face with a vengeance? Joanna Carlisle, a fifty-seven year old photojournalist, has only begun to adjust to retirement on her small ranch outside Kerrville, Texas, when she finds herself unwillingly sucked into an investigation of illegal aliens being smuggled into the United States to fill the ranks of cheap labor needed to increase corporate profits.

An unexpected visit by her former lover, Cate Hammond, and the attempted murder of their son, forces Jo to finally face what she had given up. Although she hasn't seen Cate or their son for fifteen years, she finds that the feelings she had for Cate had only been dormant, but had never died. No matter how much she fights her attraction to Cate, Jo cannot help but wonder whether she had made the right decision when she chose career and independence over love.

Reiko's Garden

Hatred…like love…knows no boundaries.

How much impact can one person have on a life?

When sixty-five-year old Callie Owen returns to her rural childhood home in Eastern Tennessee to attend the funeral of a woman she hasn't seen in twenty years, she's forced to face the fears, heartache, and turbulent events that scarred both her body and her mind. Drawing strength from Jean, her partner of thirty years, and from their two grown children, Callie stays in the valley longer than she had anticipated and relives the years that changed her life forever.

In 1949, Japanese war bride Reiko Sanders came to Frost Valley, Tennessee with her soldier husband and infant son. Callie Owen was an inquisitive ten-year-old whose curiosity about the stranger drove her to disobey her father for just one peek at the woman who had become the subject of so much speculation. Despite Callie's fears, she soon finds that the exotic-looking woman is kind and caring, and the two forge a tentative, but secret friendship.

When Callie and her five brothers and sisters were left orphaned, Reiko provided emotional support to Callie. The bond between them continued to grow stronger until Callie left Frost Valley as a teenager, emotionally and physically scarred, vowing never to return and never to forgive.

It's not until Callie goes "home" that she allows herself to remember how Reiko influenced her life. Once and for all, can she face the terrible events of her past? Or will they come back to destroy all that she loves?

Tunnel Vision

Royce Brodie, a 50-year-old homicide detective in the quiet town of Cedar Springs, a bedroom community 30 miles from Austin, Texas, has spent the last seven years coming to grips with the incident that took the life of her partner and narrowly missed taking her own. The peace and quiet she had been enjoying is shattered by two seemingly unrelated murders in the same week: the first, a John Doe, and the second, a janitor at the local university.

As Brodie and her partner, Curtis Nicholls, begin their investigation, the assignment of a new trainee disrupts Brodie's life. Not only is Maggie Weston Brodie's former lover, but her father had been Brodie's commander at the Austin Police Department and nearly destroyed her career.

As the three detectives try to piece together the scattered evidence to solve the two murders, they become convinced the two murders are related. The discovery of a similar murder committed five years earlier at a small university in upstate New York creates a sense of urgency as they realize they are chasing a serial killer.

The already difficult case becomes even more so when a third victim is found. But the case becomes personal for Brodie when Maggie becomes the killer's next target. Unless Brodie finds a way to save Maggie, she could face losing everything a second time.

Soiled Dove

In 1872, sixteen-year-old Loretta Digby fled her home in Indiana to escape an abusive step-father. Rescued from the streets of St. Joseph, Missouri by brothel owner Jack Coulter, she turns to the only work available. By twenty she became a much sought after prostitute catering to St. Jo's most influential men and dreaming of the day she can leave her past behind and start her life anew. Working with teacher, Hettie Tobias, who is traveling west for a teaching position in Trinidad, Colorado, Loretta and Amelia leave their former lives behind. In the foothills of the Sangre de Cristo Mountains outside Trinidad, Clare McIlhenney has been struggling for years to make her father's dream of owning a cattle ranch in the west come true. Working with a few ranch hands and her foreman, Ino Valdez, Clare has slowly built the ranch over the last twenty years while overcoming everything that should have stopped her.

In the spring of 1876 Loretta and her friends arrive in the dusty Colorado town. Her first meeting with Clare McIlhenney is less than inspiring. When Clare is injured, over her strenuous objections, Ino hires Loretta as a temporary cook and housekeeper for the ranch. Over the next few months, Clare struggles with her unwanted attraction to the much younger woman, unable to forget the events of her past that led to the deaths of everyone she had been close to. Determined to never lose anyone else, Clare closed off her emotions and became a distant and disliked stranger to everyone around her.

Will Loretta be able to keep her past a secret and find a new life?

Will Clare open herself up to loss yet again and put her own prejudices behind her? In a story of the struggles in a harsh and unforgiving time will the two women find peace at last?

Recipient of a 2011 award from the Golden Crown Literary Society, the premiere organization for the support and nourishment of quality lesbian literature. *Soiled Dove* won in the category of Historical Romance.

The Other Mrs. Champion

Sarah Champion, 55, of Massachusetts, was leading the perfect life with Kelley, her partner and wife of twenty-five years. That is, until Kelley was struck down by an unexpected stroke away from home. But Sarah discovers she hadn't known her partner and lover as well as she thought.

Accompanied by Kelley's long-time friend and attorney, Sarah and her children rush to Vancouver, British Columbia to say their goodbyes, only to discover another woman, Pauline, keeping a vigil over Kelley in the hospital. Confronted by the fact that her wife also has a Canadian wife, Sarah struggles to find answers to resolve heremotional and personal turmoil.

Alone and lonely, Sarah turns to the only other person who knew Kelley as well as she did—Pauline Champion. Will the two women be able to forge a friendship despite their simmering animosity? Will their growing attraction eventually become Kelley's final gift to the women she loved?

Picking Up the Pieces

Athon Dailey hasn't had many breaks in her life other than the ones she made for herself by living up to her reputation as a tough girl until she meets Lauren Shelton, a new girl at school in Duvalle, Texas. Tamed by Lauren's affection, Athon begins to believe there could be a brighter future. When Lauren's parents discover the growing relationship they send her away, making sure the two girls never have contact, leaving Athon alone and abandoned.

Twenty years later the two women meet again. Athon has established a successful military career as a helicopter pilot while Lauren has returned to Duvalle to teach. It doesn't take long for them to rekindle their feelings for one another and they finally get the chance to rebuild their teenage dreams. Permanent happiness is within their grasp when Athon's unit is deployed.

Athon comes home in a coma, diagnosed with a traumatic brain injury. She awakens to find Lauren by her side to welcome her home. When Athon chooses to retire and return to Texas, neither realizes the twists and turns the journey home will take. The Athon Dailey who returned to Lauren is not the woman she remembers. In order for their relationship to survive, Lauren begins her search for the woman she loves. Will Athon finally find her way back to Lauren and the dream they both once had? Does Lauren have the courage to live with a woman who is now a stranger?

Bringing LGBTQAI+ Stories to Life

Visit us at our website: www.flashpointpublications.com